More Than a Feline

Cat Tales & Poems

Rhys Hughes

To Linzi,

Happy 21st !

Have a great day, month, year, century & millennium...

Regards and

Best Wishes,

Rhys Hughes

Gloomy Seahorse Press

Other Titles by the Same Author

Worming the Harpy
Eyelidiad
Rawhead & Bloody Bones
The Smell of Telescopes
Stories From a Lost Anthology
Nowhere Near Milk Wood
Journeys Beyond Advice
The Percolated Stars
A New Universal History of Infamy
At the Molehills of Madness
A Sereia de Curitiba
The Crystal Cosmos
The Less Lonely Planet
The Postmodern Mariner
Engelbrecht Again!
Mister Gum
Twisthorn Bellow
The Brothel Creeper
Link Arms with Toads!
The Coandă Effect
Sangria in the Sangraal
The Truth Spinner
Tallest Stories
The Abnormalities of Stringent Strange
The Just Not So Stories
The Young Dictator

Gloomy Seahorse Press
http://rhysaurus.blogspot.com

dedicated to
Koshka

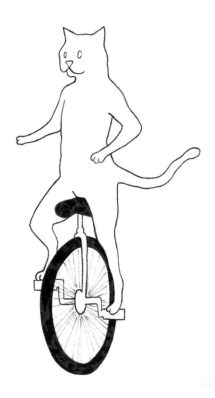

Contents

"The moon is made of cheese
and everybody knows it,
so it follows that it must attract mice,
a certain fact that is nice logic.
I really ought to go there soon;
fetch me my spacesuit and rocket!"

Foreword

Cat fiction is often considered to be twee and silly but cats are cool and therefore deserve their place in stories and poems. Some very notable authors indeed have put cats into their work: Samuel Johnson, Mikhail Bulgakov and T.S. Eliot were cat lovers, as was the arch-experimentalist William Burroughs.

Cats get everywhere in literature, as they get everywhere in rooms. Cordwainer Smith sent them into outer space and Stephen Vincent Benét had one conducting an orchestra with his tail. Lewis Carroll, Rudyard Kipling and Georges Perec were ailurophiles. Colette was equally cat crazy. Perhaps the best cat fiction ever published is the novel *I Am a Cat* by Natsume Sōseki, who is still regarded as the finest author to appear in Japan in recent centuries.

Cats are catalysing. Cats are relaxing. Cats are great!

And this is categorically true.

Cats are pillars of the community but they aren't caterpillars. Even the Pope is a Cat-holic.

I therefore feel no shame or embarrassment at now releasing a selection of my own cat stories and poems into the world. Written over a period of twenty odd years, they are what they are; which is all they can ever really be. They are paeans to our feline friends. Collected together in one volume they hopefully won't disturb the night air with the howls or hisses of their territorial disputes but get along like good passengers. Perhaps, after all, this little book is a pea-green boat, a *cat*amaran, and you, the reader, are an owl. I hope the pussycats who share the voyage make it all the way to the dry land of your enjoyment.

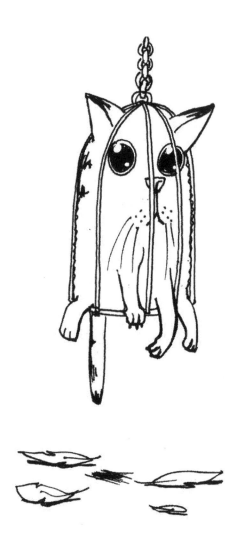

A Tale with the Title at the End

The following story is slightly unusual in that the title is at the end. Why should a title always have to be at the beginning? Why can't it be placed elsewhere? I don't mean it should just be plonked at random in the text, causing an obstruction to the characters, but positioned with due care where it hopefully can enhance the outcome.

Harrison was a successful author of fantasy books but he was having trouble with his work this morning and he sighed and put down his pen. He still wrote the old-fashioned way but this didn't mean he had a dislike of computers. He just preferred the feel of a fountain pen in his fingers. He guessed this was because he was a rock climber in his spare time, used to gripping tiny irregular swellings in the face of a cliff. He was an extremely tactile man.

The fiction he wrote wasn't the usual kind of fantasy. Harrison thought that pure escapism was a very bad thing. He loathed the idea of sedentary people with no experience of physical activity reading about dangerous journeys over appalling landscapes or about epic battles, because those readers couldn't truly understand or identify with what was happening. Harrison thought that such fantasy was fake and immature and that it pandered to losers.

So he wrote fantasy with a hard edge, a kind of fantasy that was almost the same as realism. In his fairytale castles there were always dirty dishes in the sink, and his heroes and heroines generally found themselves hampered by the mundane worries of everyday life, and his background characters were miserable and full of despair and never managed to achieve success or happiness in anything. Harrison's fantasy was the exact opposite of escapism.

He never sold many copies of his books but the critics and reviewers adored him and many imitators tried to write stories in the same way as he did. He was a famous writer in a small way and considered by a coterie of connoisseurs to be the best living exponent of this new kind of fantasy in the world. For Harrison the true enemy was Tolkien and *his* imitators because of the way he misled readers into the erroneous belief that good won in the end.

There were no simple messages about morality or anything else in the books Harrison wrote. Every incident in every one of his stories was about the difficulties of achieving any progress at all in any endeavour. His characters slogged bleakly through his tales, weighed down by a host of burdens and wearing themselves out mentally as they kept meeting obstructions that couldn't be surmounted. In fact it could be said that Harrison wrote *anti*-fantasy.

And now he was working on his latest masterpiece. So far it followed nearly the same basic pattern as his other books, heavy on the use of symbolism and with descriptive passages of unusual clarity and force. Reading a Harrison novel was at times like experiencing a particularly vivid and weird hallucination. His prose style had a crystalline quality but it was also feverish and unearthly. It was impossible to compare his work with any other living author.

He relied on a small number of powerful and effective tricks. His characters would always aspire to some great achievement, set off on a magnificent quest, but run out of energy or will or simply get distracted by the bitter ironies of life and the journey was never completed, the quest never resolved. Harrison's heroes not only had feet of clay but hearts of the same substance. They would dream of a better and more magical place which was our own world.

In this manner Harrison hoped to oppose that sloppy desire for escapism that readers of fantasy seemed to brim

10

with. His work stressed that escape of any kind at all was an illusion, an indulgence, an immature yearning that could never, and in fact *should* never, be fulfilled. And the critics were delighted and told him that he was exactly the sort of writer the public needed. He responded to such praise with a sneer because he hated to appear enthusiastic.

His fantasy worlds were often given mildly humorous names that sounded as if they were dreamy mystic places but which were only the names of fruit reversed. This convention was a private joke for Harrison. He wrote tales set in the kingdom of *Amustas*, in the republics of *Ognam* and *Ayapap*, in the anarchist communes of *Etanrgemop*, *Tiurfeparg* and *Ananab*. Very few readers ever understood that these names were jokes. Those that did felt quite smug.

Right now he was writing a new novel set on a distant planet called *Tocirpa* that orbited a star by the name of *Nolem*. But work wasn't proceeding smoothly at all. It's not that he felt blocked but that the story wanted to go in a direction that he didn't approve and he felt unable to stop it. He wrote a paragraph and then fiercely scribbled it out, so fiercely that the nib of the pen broke and he had to get out of his chair in order to fetch a new one from a cupboard.

As he returned to work with a frown on his face, his wife entered the room and softly approached him. He turned his head rapidly, his pony tail whipping his cheekbone as he did so, but the sight of her softened him. He stroked his pointed goatee beard and sighed. She came closer and asked, "What's the matter, dear? I had a feeling you were troubled, so I came to investigate. I pick up these sorts of things, you know. It's because I must be psychic."

He waved a dismissive hand, then he laughed. "Just that my new story has a life of its own. It won't do what I want it to."

"Isn't that a good thing?" she asked.

"Maybe for some other writers, yes! But not for me! Absolute control is the fundamental point of supreme importance in my working methods. For instance, I am now writing the scene where the hero of the story (though he's not a real hero, of course, as none of my characters are) is leaving our planet in a spaceship that is powered by mood-beams. He is planning to travel to *Tocirpa* and his mind must be bleak in order for him to make the ship work."

"I don't understand that."

"The spaceship engine is activated by depression and other negative moods. It won't fly if the pilot is happy. Like I said, mood-beams. So I wrote the passage in which the hero enters the ship and starts to operate the controls but then I knew that something about him was very wrong."

"What was it?" she wondered.

"It dawned on me that this character of mine was a cat! I know that sounds really silly but it's true. I mean, I ought to know better than anyone how any of my characters are going to look and act. I'm the one in charge! But somehow this cat had sneaked into my story, had taken over the role of hero and was about to travel to a distant planet before I could stop him."

"Is it really so bad for a cat to be the main character?"

"A *talking* cat!" he bellowed.

His lower lip quivered and he banged down his fist on the writing desk and for almost a minute he was unable to articulate a sensible word, then with a sigh so deep it seemed full of sunken ships, he said quietly, "Have you any idea what the critics would do to me if I published a novel about a talking cat? A novel about any sort of cat is bad enough, but one that can talk..."

"Why is it such a bad thing?"

"It's the ultimate sin, the biggest *faux pas* that any fantasy writer can ever commit! No reviewer with any credibility would ever praise a story that includes a talking cat. It's just not done. In creative writing classes where beginners are asked to write stories, do you know how many end up writing stories about cats? A heck of a lot of them! A good percentage of those stories are about cats that can talk. It's considered to be a very amateurish thing to do."

"I didn't know that," she replied.

"Well, that happens to be the case. A talking cat is a big taboo. It would be the end of my career as a serious writer."

"In that case," she suggested mildly, "don't have one."

"A career?" he shrieked.

"A cat, I meant," she explained.

"But that's just the problem!" he roared. "I can't seem to make my hero a man. He ends up being a cat, a talking cat! I must have rewritten this scene thirty or forty times and he still ends up being a talking cat. A talking cat called Tufty! Can you believe it? The critics will crucify me!"

Harrison began sobbing and his tears fell onto the page and made the ink run. "What shall I do? What shall I do?"

His wife was silent for several minutes, then she said, "I have an idea. Why don't you just write the novel with the talking cat as a hero but publish it under a false name, a pen name, a pseudonym?"

He dried his eyes and blinked at her.

A glow slowly suffused his pale hollow cheeks. His ponytail oscillated like a hairy pendulum as he wobbled his head in glee.

"Yes, yes! That will work! Yes, yes! That is a great solution. The critics will hate it but the public will love it. It means I can write the story the way it wants to be written, and make money from it too, without losing my reputation as a serious intellectual author. Thank you, thank you!"

He hugged her. She responded warmly to his embrace.

"I am so glad I married you!"

"Thanks," she said. "I am pleased about it too."

"You are the best wife a man could ever have. But I will have to think of a good pen name to use for this book."

He rested his chin on his closed hand. She waited.

Then he cried, "Why don't I just reverse my name? I could pretend my name was a piece of fruit and spell it backwards."

"*No sirrah*!" she responded.

He gaped at her and his face fell. "It's a bad idea."

She laughed. "I just made a joke. Your name backwards is 'No sirrah' and that's an old-fashioned way of saying no. Critics would work it out and it's not a proper name anyway. Why not use my name?"

"Gabrielle, you mean?"

"Sure. You are always telling me I'm like a queen to you, so why not call yourself Gabrielle Queen for this book?"

"Brilliant! And if it's successful I will write sequels."

She smiled. "Do you have a title?"

"For this one? Yes I do as a matter of fact." He rummaged through all the papers scattered over his desk until he found the first page of his manuscript. He took his new pen and scratched out the original title. Then he blinked his eyes a few times rapidly as he gathered his thoughts.

His darling wife purred and nuzzled up against him as with one hand he stroked her furry pointed ears and with the other wrote the following three words, which also happen to be the real title of *this* story:

His Wife's Whiskers

The Cat

"We'll have to get him neutered," Judy had said that morning. And yet now, outstretched on his favourite sofa, he seemed to be at ease. Perhaps he had not fully understood the consequences of her words. His eyes were half-closed and his breathing was shallow.

The sound of footsteps on the gravel of the driveway roused him from his daydreams. They were talking about 'the cat' again, the problems involved in keeping animals. The deeper voice belonged to the vet. The jangling keys were like icicles melting in the sun.

The cat rose and stretched himself. He yawned and padded his way over to Stephen's lap. For some reason, he seemed even more lethargic than usual. He curled up and settled down once more. Stephen said nothing.

He remembered vaguely how Judy and her friend, Angela, had stood above him, calmly discussing his fate. He had not associated the subject of their talk with himself. He had thought their victim was to be one smaller than he, younger.

"He's a little too old now, isn't he?" Angela had been concerned.

"Yes, but I know a vet who will do it." Judy had smiled, showing her perfect white teeth. "As a personal favour."

The cat shifted uneasily. His ears twitched as the front door opened. But he didn't move. He felt almost paralysed, as if frozen by the glare of headlights on a lonely country road.

"There he is!" Judy's voice was firm and merciless.

The vet placed his bag on the table and frowned. "I shouldn't really be doing this, you know."

"He's been making smells." Angela reached down to

15

stroke the cat. "All over the house."

"He will struggle." The vet drew out a scalpel. "You will have to hold him down."

"Don't worry." Judy grinned. "We drugged his food."

The cat gazed up at the bright point of steel. Judy and Angela loomed closer. With a mighty effort, he leapt up and bounded across the room, through the hallway, into the kitchen and out through the cat flap.

Even from the safety of the garden, he could hear Stephen's screams.

Cat in a Balloon

No Moses this:
his basket floats on currents
of air;
neutered aeronaut
huffing alone,
fur bristling, hissing
pink tongue far
                from home

Bored with cupboards,
secret gardens
and under the bed,
he seeks out new lands;
exotic feasts
of old golden birds
and mice of
                the East

Making a Feline

When Harold felt sick he went to the bathroom and released the pain both ways. And then he sat on the toilet seat smoking and talking to his cat, who was also called Harold and who didn't exist.

"You know something," said Harold. "I've been thinking."

"What about?" asked Harold.

"Well,| said Harold, |maybe it's time I gave up drinking on my own and made a few friends. Just one or two. We could walk in the park and they could talk and I could nod and even listen."

"I'm not sure that's a good idea," replied Harold. He thought about it carefully. He rolled the thought on his tongue and spat it out. "No I really don't think that would be suitable. After all you're hardly the sort of person anyone would want to go to the park with."

"What do you mean?" cried Harold. "Haven't I got the right to have a friend the same as everybody else! What are you getting at?"

"It's not a question of rights," answered Harold calmly. "We've all got rights. It's more a question of standards."

Grumbling, Harold took another swig and lit a gnarled cigarette. Blue smoke curled the question-mark for him. "Who are you to give me advice anyway. You're just jealous. Perhaps you're scared I'll leave you if I find a friend. A friend of my very own." Harold began to cry. "I've made all the wrong choices in life."

"Don't blubber." Harold covered his ears. "I hate it when you blubber. Can't stand moaning, moaning. What is there to complain about really? Life is supposed to be absurd.

Whatever you do you'll regret it. Kierkegaard said so. If you do something you'll regret it and if you don't do it you'll also regret it. That's what he said. True enough."

"What do you mean?" cried Harold again. "What would you know about Kierkegaard. You're just a cat. A cat. Besides you don't need much company. A ball of string is enough for you. Well, it's not enough for me. Do you hear. Not good enough for me. What sort of company is a ball of string!" Harold's voice became a shriek.

"I know the meaning of despair as well as you. It's not all play. I've got problems too. You wouldn't believe what I have to put up with some days."

"Damn right I wouldn't," sneered Harold.

"You're so full of self-pity," countered Harold. "You ooze with it. I don't like you," he suddenly decided.

Harold turned grey. "Well you can find a new home if that's your attitude."

"It's not my attitude," replied Harold. "Listen." And he told a tale. "A man's hat blew off in the wind and a dog ate it, but the dog's owner absolutely refused to apologise. Dogs will be dogs, he said."

"So what?" demanded Harold.

"Wait for it," sighed Harold. "You should learn to be a little more patient. Well, this man said dogs will be dogs and the owner of the hat said I don't like your attitude and the dog owner said it's not my *'at 'e chewed*, it's yours."

"Ha, ha!" Harold's mouth laughed but upside-down. "Anyway I don't care whether you like me or not. You're unhygienic. You leave hairs in the bed and tongue tracks in the butterdish."

"You hypocrite." Harold shook his head in disbelief. "You haven't had a bath in four months. You haven't washed your hair for over a year."

"Natural oils," responded Harold.

18

When Harold felt better he flushed the cigarette butt down the bowl, took another swig and stumbled out of the bathroom. A queue had formed, each silent bladder swollen with fury. The first in line dived into the room and gagged on the stench. "You dirty old bastard," he called back.

You dirty old bastard, Harold thought speculatively as he shuffled on the threadbare ochre carpet to his room. Old newspapers yellowed the floor. He reached out for the tarnished brass knob. Damp cabbage odours rushed to kiss his overlong nose.

Once inside Harold lost no time in wringing the bon from the mot. "You dirty old bastard," he echoed.

"Shut up," cried Harold. "Shut up." He clenched teeth and raised fists. "Shut up, shut up." He collapsed to the edge of the bed wheezing.

There was a knock on the door. "What's that noise?" came a voice.

Harold rolled his eyes. "The landlord," he cried. "Quick under the bed!"

"Rent day," came the voice again with another knock. Harold darted under the bed.

"And stay there," Harold hissed.

"Open up, open up, rent day," the voice repeated.

Harold opened the door and stood there with an attempt at a smile. Mr Grasp eyed Harold with jovial suspicion. His gold necklace and bracelet glittered in the shadows. "Rent day," he echoed. Harold nodded. His hands were constantly moving, seeking solace in his thinning hair, beneath each armpit. "Well, aren't you going to invite me in?"

"Come in, come in," said Harold.

His bottle was safe in the deeps of his pocket. He wore his dressing gown inside-out to conceal this pocket. "Have you just got up?" asked Mr Grasp. "Don't you know what time it is? It's the middle of the afternoon."

19

"I've been ill," lied Harold. And then he blew his nose on his sleeve, rather self-consciously as if truth should out.

"I see," Mr Grasp wrinkled up his face. "What's that bloody awful smell?" He cocked his head at Harold. "You haven't been keeping animals have you," he asked. "You know the rules about pets."

"Of course," stuttered Harold. "No, never, never."

"NO PETS," said Mr Grasp in capital letters. Harold looked down to where Mr Grasp's foot was an inch from the bed. Harold's tail was poking out. Harold decided to change the subject.

"Look here," he said, "what about fixing the light in the hallway. It's dangerous at night, you know. Pitch bloody dark like treacle. Swimming through the dark. Groping."

Mr Grasp frowned. "And what would you be doing coming in at night," he demanded. And then he laughed. "You've got no reason to be out at all. You're a sad specimen of humanity." He paused lovingly. "Now pay me."

Harold unwound his cheque book all curled up in the biscuit tin on the mantelpiece. He sucked the tip of his ballpoint pen for no good reason and wrote out the cheque. He was buying time again. He handed the piece of paper to Mr Grasp ever so gingerly. "It's all smudged," complained Mr Grasp. But he took it and made comic bouncing motions.

After he had gone, Harold bent down on hands and knees and peered under the bed. "It's alright now, it's safe. You can come out." But Harold had fallen asleep. "He's gone you daft bugger," said Harold. Harold yawned and stretched and opened his green eyes. He came out reluctantly, his tail sweeping the parameters of his annoyance.

They sat by the window, staring through the grimy glass at the overgrown garden below. Weak sun reflected off the slates of exhausted houses. Harold stared at a seagull on a chimney. His jaws chattered. "What shall we do now?"

"Let's go to the park," Harold suggested.

"Not again," cried Harold.

"Oh, come on," pleaded Harold.

"But it's getting dark, the nights are drawing in."

"Please," begged Harold.

"All right then," Harold tutted and jumped down licking himself once.

"We could try to talk to some people there," Harold said. "We could try to make a friend." He scratched his head. "Let me get dressed."

Harold waited impatiently. "Come on you old fool."

"Just a moment," replied Harold. He frowned. "Now promise you won't run away," he insisted. "Promise you won't get stuck up any trees."

Harold sighed. "I promise," he said.

Cat in a Bathysphere

Nose pressed hard to foot-thick
glass, he eyes the uglies of
the deep:
glistening octopus, rubbery
squid, lantern fish and
nameless ones.
Out of reach delicacies
drifting past his gaze;
whiskers twitch, jaws chatter
a scowl appears
O! The unfairness of water!

Cat o' Nine Tales

Herodotus, the old grey cat with a mouth full of stories, usually comes into my kitchen in the evenings. I may be sucking soup from a ladle, juggling mangoes, chopping off the tails of mice (good spaghetti is hard to come by these days) but I always have time for him. For Herodotus is not a cat to be trifled with; and when his mouth is indeed full of stories it is wise to let him spit them out. Else he will swallow them and probably be sick over the lasagne.

Not that anyone would notice. I keep a kitchen so spotlessly dirty that even the drunken pirates and roughnecks who frequent my restaurant are satisfied. They will often remark that my bootlace-and-green-gravy pizza was absolutely disgusting and then pat me on the back for it and throw me a coin encrusted with teeth where other sailors (doubtless scurvy fellows) were foolish enough to test its validity. The teeth I place under my pillow at night; the coins I give to Herodotus. What he does with them is anyone's guess.

He is indeed an unusual cat. As with most felines, he was born with no less than nine lives, though he has done his best to reduce this number. Sometimes I will baste a vole for him, or grill a dogfish, while he relates his adventures with a slow languid wink in the smoky light of the charcoal ovens. Often we will share a bottle of Chablis or dip our tongues into the sherry syllabub and talk about old times and bewail a world that has changed far too much.

My kitchen is small and dark and its warped wooden timbers are a record of all the meals I have ever prepared. The stains form a pattern that is my history. Spices and sweat, the yellowing effect of turmeric and tears. Through the single grimy window I can glimpse the wan phosphorescence of seaweed-draped ghost ships smuggling illicit spirits between the darkened islands of the bay. Against the walls of my kitchen, I can hear the slap of the harbour waters. And always Herodotus comes, snatching words from an unknown place, to scratch the claws of his life on the itch of my days.

My restaurant is now more popular than ever with the buccaneers and privateers of the port, who sing strange songs as they gorge themselves on my food and empty my beer barrels of their muddy contents. We can always hear their jabbering, even above the hissings and bubblings of my pots and pans. They are slimy scoundrels to a man and woman; swarthy, bristly, leering and jeering rogues, scourges of obscure compass points, bright blue with lewd tattoos. But Herodotus remains unimpressed by such patrons. He merely casts a sardonic eye at their antics through a hole in the door which leads to the eating area. And then he turns back and idly licks a paw.

"Giovanni," he says. "Why don't you sell-up and open a new place in the town centre? There are many tourists there, with bulging purses. But these pirates leave abominable tips. And they smell. It is important to plan for the future..."

"A slow steady business," I reply, throwing down my cleaver and mopping my forehead with a pancake. "Besides, blackguards make good customers in other ways. Their tastebuds have all been ruined by rum and tobacco. Where else could I serve worm curry with a side-order of nettles and not receive complaints?"

At which, Herodotus always shrugs his shoulders and sighs. As far as he is concerned, I am somewhat lacking in ambition. To forestall further chiding, I attempt to change the subject. I say: "Tell me about your nine lives and how you lost eight of them. I've always wanted to know the details. You've kept making hints and allusions, but these don't satisfy any more. How exactly did you die each time and what did it feel like?"

Herodotus yawns and leaps up onto the edge of a huge black cauldron suspended over the fire. Hedgehog and red lentil soup boils and seethes. "I was about to tell you the story of Tina Wertigo, the gyroscope girl, and her unbalanced liaison with the Mad Twist. In return for her favours he offered her blue-rugs, ambergris and onion-domes..."

"Come down from there. You'll burn yourself!" I cry. "Or at the very least, you'll singe your tail." But Herodotus ignores me and merely yawns once more. He is a stubborn, as well as reckless, sort of cat, which partly explains why he lost eight of his nine lives in such quick succession. "Besides, I'd rather hear about yourself."

"Why don't you keep quiet and listen then?" Herodotus manages to keep his balance on the lip of the cauldron. "If you really want to know about my other lives I'll tell you. But you mustn't interrupt!"

Now it is my turn to sigh. With remarkable dexterity, I begin to wash and stack the dirty dishes at the sink. They quickly pile into a tower which teeters alarmingly every time I add another piece of crockery. Ten dishes, twenty, thirty. My scrubbing brush flicks soapy water into the furthest corners of the room. I am deeply shamed by Herodotus' rebuke and seek the redemption of mindless toil.

"I lost my first life in a mangle. I fell into a washtub and was stirred with a wooden pole, lifted out with a pair of tongs and squeezed between the rollers until my yellow eyes popped. That was in the city of Skour, where every day is washday and the people yearn constantly to erase from their souls the blemish of some half-remembered sin. Thus Skour is a city in a constant state of flux, each day stripping away the surface layer of dirt and time to reveal another city yet more dirty. The mangles were powered by an elaborate system of windmills and once trapped in their jaws there was nothing I could do. What did it feel like? Oh, like the thought of rain on a sunny day..."

All this while, I am washing and stacking dishes and the tower is growing taller and taller. I do not doubt the truth of Herodotus' tales, for I have never known him attempt to deceive me. Indeed, he is usually more restrained than I would like him to be. Adding cups and saucers to my pagoda of plates, I ask: "Wasn't it more painful than that?"

Herodotus narrows his eyes and stares at me for a long minute. Who can tell what he is thinking? He crouches on the very edge of the black cauldron and his whiskers curl and droop in the clouds of steam that billow from the pot in fitful asthmatic gasps. Swathed by this aromatic mist, he resembles a tired moon sinking slowly into the white madness of a stormy sea; the horses that live beneath the waves are snorting and foaming at the mouth.

"I lost my second life in a mirror. That was in the house of an old lady whose hair was piled up on her head with a selection of multicoloured knitting needles. Her mirror ran slow; it reflected a more distant past as the future stretched out before it. Thus she was able to witness herself as a young girl again, unlined but still unloved, moving with the sure grace of a cloud. In this mirror I saw my own origins, my ultimate demise in the womb of my mother. But reality, it turned out, was nothing more than this; it was myself who was the reflection. Death had claimed me before life. It felt like a sore thumb without the pain..."

At this, I frown and attempt a wry smile, without success. Such an odd, metaphysical sort of death is quite beyond my understanding. I begin to suspect that Herodotus is falling back on metaphors to express what in all probability was a rather mundane death. "You were appalled at the prospect of losing your youth and the shock killed you?" I suggest. Herodotus blinks and lets loose a dry chuckle, utterly devoid of humour.

"No, the mirror fell on me..."

Here I shudder, while Herodotus closes his mouth, as evil as a shark's, and recalls the chuckle that had threatened to slip into a huge great guffaw. Abruptly, he raises his tail, curls it round and licks the tip once. When he resumes, he eyes me with a disturbing curiosity, as if he is seeing me for the first time.

"I lost my third life in a market. This was in the Thirsty Desert, where nomads mounted on camels vainly attempted to catch swallows and where enormous salamanders vainly attempted to swallow nomads. Anyway, no sooner had I set foot upon this sandy waste in my travels, than my guide, a crafty fellow with a blue turban, turned on me and trussed me up. He carried me across the desert for three days and three nights, his unwound turban trailing behind him like a portable river, until we reached a town whose houses were made out of blocks of salt. There was a market in this town which dealt in camel's milk cheese, slaves and fur. I was skinned and made into a pair of slippers for the Sultana of Prune. It felt like a short hop on a long pier..."

"The other way round surely?" I retort, but Herodotus shakes his head. He knows exactly what he is about, this cat, and resents my need to strike a note of sense on the anvil of his nostalgia.

"I lost my fourth life in a river. At the top of a cobbled alley in the port town of Ezbyx, I chanced upon a barrel of yoghurt. I licked my way to the centre and then became stuck. My frantic attempts to free myself toppled the barrel and it rolled, grumbling and bouncing, all the way down the street, faster and faster, over the side of the quay and into the water. It sank instantly, with me inside, and the fish that poked their heads into my watery coffin later were astonished to see an old enemy so caught out by his own greed. That one felt like the taste of lemons at dawn; a sour end before a fresh start..."

I refrain from remarking that this was an absurd lack of foresight on his part. I do not wish to upset Herodotus further at this stage. I merely continue to stack dishes, two by two, higher and higher and higher.

"I lost my fifth life in a long fall. In the mighty city of Abarak, home of the Mad Twist, stands the Tower of Unlikely Dimensions. This is a structure so high that those who stand at the very top can see the curvature of the globe. Well, you can guess what happened. I fell and span towards the ground. As I sped past them, people on different levels offered me a stroke or a kind word or a piece of cheese. I eventually died of old age just before striking the ground. It felt like a song played on an untuned piano..."

I lower my head; there is nothing more to say.

"I lost my sixth and seventh lives at the same instant. This is what happened. While working as a sorcerer's apprentice, I learnt the secret of protecting myself by magical arts while I slept. I painted mystic symbols on my eyelids which would kill any assassin who looked upon them. One day, the sorcerer left two crystal balls on the table in his chamber. One could show the past; the other could show the future. When I took a furtive look at them, I died twice. One of the crystals showed me fast asleep the previous day; the other showed me fast asleep the following day. So I was slain by my own cunning. It felt like sitting on a chair warmed by another occupant. It felt like a sneeze in a paper bag..."

I puff out my cheeks and mutter to myself. The crockery is piled so high that it nearly touches the ceiling. But I continue to add more and Herodotus continues to perch on the edge of the cauldron, while the soup blows scalding bubbles and the pirates in the restaurant yell and growl. My mutter is a quiet one; a rustle like the sound of leaves spinning through the air or like sand that is being poured over an original idea.

"I lost my eighth life in a garret. It felt like a criticism of the sun. I moved into a crumbling deserted house and slept right at the very top. This was in a town where all the avenues are treeless but scattered with rose petals. I became a poet, sleeping during the day, as usual, but taking long walks through cemeteries at night. My poems were rejected and I had to pay for their publication myself. Few copies were sold and I began to starve. Naturally, like all good poets, I swallowed a phial of poison and died in my basket..."

At last I have finished. The dishes form a pillar of dripping discs that push against the weight of the ceiling. I am exhausted. I nod to Herodotus and leave the kitchen by the back door. At the jetty, I pause and gaze out to sea, wiping my hands on my filthy apron. I need to breathe some fresh air before turning to my next task.

As I stand, there is a crash and a yowl from the kitchen. I presume that some of the roughnecks have started a fight. I roll my tired eyes in exasperation and turn around to go back. Herodotus is standing by my feet, hissing and scowling.

"That was very rude of you," he says. "I haven't finished yet. I haven't told you about how I lost my ninth life..."

"Don't be ridiculous! How could you have lost that? Cats only have nine. You'd be a ghost now if you had..."

Herodotus does not reply. I peer more closely at him in the gloom. There is something different about him. I cannot fathom it. Finally the truth dawns. I clear my throat nervously.

"Well?"

"I lost my ninth life in a kitchen. I used to visit a warty old fool who owned a disgusting restaurant. I used to tell him tales. But he was too much of a dullard to appreciate them. One evening, I was balancing on a cauldron of boiling soup and this imbecile was stacking dishes into an enormous pile. Abruptly, he turned around and left the kitchen, slamming the door behind him. The vibration knocked the tower of dishes down onto me and I fell into the soup..."

Autumn Cat

Rumpus was an autumn cat,
his ears would turn yellow
then red, then brown
and fall off his head onto the ground.
But the following spring
they would grow back again.

Rimsky's the Limit

Rimsky was a business cat
but he had no suit
and had no hat. Nonetheless
he knew what he was about
when he told his bold
colleagues how to act
without fear in the
big wide commercial sphere.

They ran a factory
those industrial felines
and dominance was their motivation.
No other kitties throughout the nation
were quite as ruthless
or half as lethal
despite their purrs
as Rimsky's gang of profiteers.

Hostile takeovers and mergers
increased their assets yearly
and Rimsky grew less surly
and licked his fangs in sheer delight
as every deal he struck went right
for his furry people
all of whom were other cats
who loved to win.

By charging less than his rivals
he undercut them drastically
and forced them into bankruptcy
until his firm was the only one

among the few left in credit.
"Rimsky is a bandit. To rack and ruin
he has driven us!" they all said it
and it was perfectly true.

Dog biscuits was the product
that Rimsky's empire was based on
and when he had a monopoly
he changed the ingredients
to summarise his power.
A few drops of poison in the flour
and the greatest dream
of every feline was realised.

The dogs they died one by one
across the land. Such fun for Rimsky
and his friends, that merry band,
to witness the harrowing ends
of mongrels and pedigrees alike.
A joyous and uplifting sight
to crown their delight as they
walked around the dogless towns.

Dog and bird who hear these words
take care to guard your skin.
Beware of fat sinful cats
devoted to the profit margin!

Fat Cat Fable

Let me repeat a story I once heard about two cats who hung out every day at a place called Bar Humbug. It was a café for cats. The two felines who practically lived there were a pair of friends from way back when. Have you ever been to way back when? No, I haven't either, and I don't even know where it is or what the terrain is like. I'm a forest cat myself.

One of the cats was bigger than the other. In fact he was about one and a half times the size of his friend. Whenever they ordered a bowl of food from the waitress who came to take their order, the same little argument would begin and it was never settled. This was the one thing they disagreed on. Apart from this, I don't think they ever swiped at each other.

Most cats have territorial disputes and battles because of pride and vanity, but this pair argued only about portions, the exact amounts that should be shared between them. It might seem to you that the obvious solution would be for them to order their food separately and pay for it individually, so each could have the quantity they needed and pay for no extra.

But that's an impolite and antisocial way of doing things. In Bar Humbug such behaviour is discouraged most severely. In fact it is banned. The point of this café is to promote harmony and solidarity among felines and to get them to realise they can be more successful in the world if they work together. All food therefore is served in one dish and only one.

I guess that if two humans were presented with an identical situation the first impulse would be to divide the food in half. I can hear the words "Half for you, half for me" in my mind as I picture the scene. But cats think more deeply than that. The larger cat insisted that an equal portion was unfair to him because a bigger physique required more nourishment.

This was perfectly logical. A giant can't be expected to survive and thrive on the same amount of sustenance that would be adequate for a fairy. The bigger cat put it like this, "I am 50% larger than you, so I need two thirds of the food in the bowl and you only need one third." But the smaller cat thought that this was very bad arithmetic and he replied as follows:

"I want half the food for myself but I understand that you need an extra quarter of a bowl to eat the equivalent of my half. So I am willing to let you eat three fifths of the bowl while I only have two fifths. I think you'll find that these calculations are more correct than yours. Let's apply my system to the next bowl of food we order and see how we get along."

The bigger cat agreed to the suggestion and the following day, when they went to Bar Humbug, they applied to their mouths the ratios that the smaller cat had worked out. When the meal was finished they were both slightly hungry and dissatisfied but neither of them complained. Not yet at any rate. The truth is that they were nearly always hungry. Like all cats.

Every day this routine was followed and gradually it became apparent that the bigger cat was growing bigger and the smaller cat was getting thinner. Soon the bigger cat was exactly twice as large as his companion and during one meal he said to his friend, "I am sorry but the way things are done needs to change. I can't live on the portion I am now receiving."

"But you are eating half again as much as I am."

"Yes but I am *twice* as bulky as you! It is obvious that the ratios need to be adjusted to take account of this fact.

From this moment hence, I will devour two thirds of the bowl and you only one third."

This time the bigger cat's arithmetic was indisputable and the smaller cat had no choice but to concur with the sums. And so all future meals were shared out in a different manner, with the fatter cat taking twice what was allotted to his skinnier comrade. But hunger still remained and it did so because of the bigger cat's greed and the smaller cat's deprivation.

The months passed and eventually the larger cat grew no less than thrice the size of the other. And so the proportions were adjusted yet again. The fatter cat ate three quarters of the bowl and his friend was only given one quarter. The results of this change were drastic and inevitable. The bigger cat kept increasing his size while the smaller kept decreasing his.

The staff at Bar Humbug saw what was happening but it wasn't really up to them to interfere. The café was run by an old fellow called Scrooge who never did anything to change the course of destiny. He hadn't even bothered changing his name to that of a more pleasant character. So the big cat and the little cat had no help from that quarter, nor did they want it.

Time passed, as it has a habit of doing, and within a few years the bigger cat was taking nine tenths of the food in the bowl. The smaller cat was so thin he could hardly be seen from the front or back. It was almost as if the fat cat was a kind of fluffy vampire, expanding at the expense of his friend and absorbing his substance into his own, feeding on him from afar.

One afternoon, the bigger cat strolled into Bar Humbug and gave his usual order. "Solitary diners are not permitted in this café," he was told, but he simply shook his head and replied, "I am not alone but with a friend." And the waitress heard faint purring coming from the thin air beside him, so they showed him to a table and served him the bowl of food he wanted.

He devoured all of it, every single morsel, and even licked the bowl clean at the end. Then he got up and left, saying, "It is always so much more pleasant to share a meal with friends than to eat alone." And when the staff checked they found two sets of footprints leading out of the building. That is the story exactly as I heard it and I have changed not a single word.

The moral of this tale is that fairness is sometimes unfair when taken to its logical conclusion. The fact that this tale has a moral means it is a fable. A fable is supposed to provide food for thought and personally I think this one has done that. Food for thought is an important resource to supply. Not only does a belly know hunger. Reason and imagination know hunger too.

The reason I tell stories is because it is nicer to share them rather than keep them to myself. So I suggest we share this one equally, half and half. I have told it and now you can read it. What is that you are saying? You are larger than me and so require more for the sake of fairness? I find it hard to believe you are larger than me but it would be churlish to argue.

You want to take two thirds of the story and leave one third to me? How much larger than me are you? I see. That is bad mathematics. I am willing to let you have three fifths and I will take two fifths. What do you say to that? Let us meet tomorrow and I will tell a new tale and we can apply the suggested ratios to it and see what happens. It might not end so badly.

Silky Salathiel

Silky Salathiel was a travelling cat
with the taste of the Orient on the tip of his tongue.
He had wandered the streets of Mandalay
enticed by the scents of ginger and lime;
where the oldest songs are sung
in the Rub-Al-Khali
he had scratched at the rugs in Bedouin tents.

I knew him well when I was young.
We sailed the Brahmaputra in an old sea-chest,
lived in a basket in Kathmandu,
climbed the mountains of the Hindu Kush,
bathed in fountains of milk in Xanadu,
and I was the friend whom he loved best;
the oldest fish in the Caspian Sea.

But of course I lived longer than him
(now he is gone memories are all that remain).
He was not just a cat but a travelling cat
who had danced flamenco in the castles of Spain,
licked the cheese in shady Provence,
and drunk the ale in the snowy Ukraine.
Silky Salathiel the travelling cat
with the taste of the East on the tip of his tongue
and that of the West on the tip of his tail.

Lady, Tiger and Protozoon

I like telling stories, but I dislike explaining them. So you can work this one out for yourself. And while you ponder over its meaning, I will creep up the spiral staircase, climb into bed and blow the candle out...

Once there was a semi-barbaric King who had a beautiful daughter. So beautiful was she that mirrors held their breath and chocolate eggs hatched in her presence. Yet she was a fiercely jealous woman with a cruel streak. Her hair was the darkest shade of red and her teeth were like the bars of a cage.

Although this Princess had many rich suitors, she rejected them all in favour of a poor poet who had once recited some verses at Court. Naturally, her father would hear nothing of her marrying a commoner. He forbade them to meet, and when they disobeyed his command, he had the poet arrested.

Now the King had a strange way in which to try criminals. They would be led into an arena with two doors set into the walls. Behind one of the doors waited a young girl; behind the other paced a ravenous tiger. The defendant had to choose which door to open. If he chose the girl, he had to marry her and provide for her future. There is little need to mention what would happen if he chose the tiger...

As we all know, a tiger is a cat, and that's why this tale has been included in this book of cat stories, but it's not the sort of cat you would want to stroke behind the ears or tickle on the tummy. Not unless you were some kind of gigantic bear or ape, and even then you might think twice.

Anyway, to return to what I was saying, the evening before the trial, the Princess managed to get a message to the cell where her lover languished. She promised to find out what lay behind each door and to indicate the correct one with a signal. At this, the poet did not cheer up. He remembered the strength of her jealousy. It was possible she would rather see him eaten than engaged to a rival.

The next morning, as he stepped out into the arena, true to her word, the Princess pointed at one of the doors. Reluctantly, he stepped forward, grasped the handle and pulled. He had decided that it was better to trust the woman he loved than his own judgement...

A few weeks later, a vizier from a distant land, a man with a blue turban wrapped around his head like a spiral of smoke, arrived at the Court. His master wished to become a suitor of the Princess. The King told him everything I have just told you, but no more. Yet the vizier insisted on knowing the rest. He wanted to know what had come out of the door. Had it been the lady or the tiger?

The King was troubled by this request, but had no desire to offend the vizier, so he led him up to a secret chamber. Guarded by a savage dog with a purple tongue, a microscope stood on a table, proof of the King's interest in science. The King fitted a glass slide under the lens and beckoned for the vizier to look through the eyepiece.

"That is an amoeba," said the King. "A protozoon of ever-changing shape. As the amoeba can divide into two wholes, so can the ending of my tale. I will answer your question in two different ways. It is up to you to choose the ending you think is correct."

The vizier was puzzled by the King's attitude, but he nodded his head and waited to hear what the King had to say. The King moved to the window and gazed out across the Palace gardens. Peacocks screeched from the battlements and unicorns raced each other around the flowerbeds.

"It was the girl who stood behind the door. She came out and the poet embraced her. She was very beautiful. But when he tried to kiss her, she slapped him across the cheek. Her beauty lay only on the outside. As he stumbled backwards, she slapped him again. And when he opened his mouth to protest, she slapped him a third time.

"Their life together was not happy. She threw his poems out of the window, into the river, and forced him to do all the housework. Her habits began to repulse him. She was fond of eating raw meat. His only friend was a cat named Kismet. When Kismet vanished one night and he found traces of fur around the mouth of his new wife, he was filled with despair.

"The following day, his boots were discovered outside the tiger's cage in the Royal Zoo. It was assumed that he had climbed over the railings and fed himself to the half-starved beast. It was widely believed that he was driven to this ironic end by his domestic troubles. At any rate, he was never seen again."

The King paused and turned back to the vizier. The vizier held his nose and wept tears onto the King's plush carpets. "A tragic ending," he sobbed. His tears fell in such torrents that the fleas on the King's dog climbed up them to his face. While he cried, a golden chariot pulled by eagles flew past the window and the sun and moon danced in their orbits. But the tears obscured these marvels from his vision.

"That was merely the first ending," replied the King. "Actually, it was the tiger that stood behind the door in the arena. It came out and the poet turned pale. He began to recite a death-poem he had composed the previous night. It was a very unusual poem and it charmed the tiger. When the poet opened his mouth to recite another verse, it licked his face and lay down at his feet.

"Because of this turn of events, his life was spared. However, the tiger was condemned to death for failing in its duty. The poet felt obliged to rescue the tiger. He visited the

Royal Zoo and attempted to force the lock of its cage. Unfortunately, he was too weak. He needed to obtain the keys. To do this, he approached the daughter of the zookeeper.

"The following day, his boots were discovered outside the bedroom of the daughter. She had seduced him and he had fallen asleep. When he woke up, it was too late. The tiger had gone. Tortured by his conscience, he went mad and hung himself from the rafters in his attic."

At these words, the vizier wailed and gnashed his teeth. He did not want to choose between these endings, but he knew in his heart that it was impossible not to choose. Even if he chose not to choose, he would still be making a choice. In time, he did indeed select the right ending, and led his camel back to his own land, his unwound turban trailing behind him like a portable river in the sands of time.

But now it is your turn to choose. One of these endings is true, but which? Well, let me give you a clue. We all know that a leopard can never change its spots. But can a tiger change its stripes? And more to the point, would it ever want to?

Goodnight...

The Cellar Door

Miranda was delighted. "The house has been transformed into a grotto," she said. Lucien frowned at her. They sat huddled around a single candle. Barely ten minutes ago, he had been standing in the shower. Droplets of water still glistened in his hair.

"I don't like power cuts," he announced. When the lights had failed, he had fumbled for his towel and had lurched out of the bathroom. His pride was still damaged from where he had slipped on the soap. He was feeling decidedly petulant.

"Nonsense!" Miranda smiled. "You don't mean to tell me you're afraid of the dark? I can't believe it!"

"But everything seems different. I mean, look at the cellar door! It appears slightly sinister, as if something is going to come out of it."

"I suppose you're right. Yes, I see what you're getting at. Indeed, I'm convinced that something *will* come out of it before very long, although I'm not entirely sure what."

Lucien blinked. "Eh?" He had expected Miranda to dismiss his fears as groundless, to keep him safe in the security of her scepticism. Instead, he was now faced with the task of comforting himself. He had no choice but to retract his statement.

"This is ridiculous!" he cried. "What could possibly come out of the cellar door? You are letting your imagination run amok. There is nothing down there anyway. I refuse to discuss the matter further."

"Now you are just being brave." Miranda shook a finger. "You are trying to keep me calm for my own sake. It is very sweet of you, but also very wrong. You must admit the truth. We both know that something will come out of the cellar door and that, whatever it is, it will certainly be very

41

terrible."

Lucien rolled his eyes in alarm. He had lost control of the situation. As usual, Miranda had taken over. His only option now was to brazen it out.

"In that case, if you are so sure, perhaps you would care to make a bet? I say that nothing will come out of the cellar door, and I am prepared to put my money where my mouth is!"

"Oh yes?" Miranda raised an eyebrow. "Then I accept. However, I can think of a far more interesting stake than money."

"Well?" Lucien was growing cold. He shivered and glowered at the same time. "What is it?"

"If I win, then you must do all the housework for a whole month!"

Lucien froze. This was a prospect that chilled the very marrow in his bones. He rubbed his clammy palms together and gasped for breath. But a sudden idea came to him. He began to see how he could outdo even these cruel terms.

"Very well. But if I win, you must finally introduce me to your friends. You must introduce me as your lover and you must inform them that I am ten years younger than you."

Miranda smiled a thin smile. He had found the only chink in her defence. "Humph!" she said. But there was no turning back. She could not afford to lose face in front of him.

They sat in silence, both watching the cellar door. As he gazed with wide eyes, trying not to blink, Lucien realised how advantageous his position was. If something did come out of the cellar door, and if it was as terrible as Miranda had predicted, it was unlikely it would leave him in any fit state to do housework. In essence, he could not lose.

He therefore felt less reluctant about imagining what sort of something could emerge from such a cellar door at such a time. It was certainly an unlovely cellar door: it needed a lick of paint and a new lock. And the cellar it guarded was a miserable hole. Miranda was incapable of appreciating this fact. She had never once been down there. He, however, knew it well.

They had only moved into the house a month before. As far as all her friends were concerned, Miranda had moved in alone. Their affair was still secret. Miranda was not only embarrassed by the age difference, but also wished to preserve her independent image. She liked to pretend she had no need of men. Consequently, whenever they had a visitor, Lucien had to stay safely out of the way. The cellar had been Miranda's choice.

It was a dank cellar, and an unpleasant place of confinement, but he had never been aware of any evil presence down there with him. On the contrary, if any ghosts had shared his hiding place then they were of the benevolent sort. Perhaps the ghost of the old cat that had lived in the house before them was one. By all accounts it had been a pleasant creature.

"He led a happy life, didn't he?" Lucien said suddenly.

"Who?" Miranda frowned.

"The old cat. He came to a peaceful end at a great age, loved by all who knew him. No problems there, were there?"

"None at all." Miranda agreed with such alacrity that Lucien started in shock. Miranda usually argued every point. The fact that she had not contradicted him meant she was insincere. She was hiding something.

"But perhaps he only pretended to be nice," he ventured. "Perhaps, underneath, he was bitter, twisted and insane."

Miranda did not reply. This was firm evidence that he was on the right track. As he thought about it more carefully, he decided that there *had* been an evil essence down there with him. Yes, there was no doubt about it: he had felt icy breath on the nape of his neck.

"He hates us," he said, "because we have taken over his house. We have invaded his privacy. There is nowhere left for his ghost to hide now except the cellar. And he is not even safe down there. Every so often, I disturb his peace by tramping down the steps."

He rubbed his jaw. "Perhaps he wasn't a harmless old cat at all. Perhaps he was a demon. Yes, that's it! He had a malevolent gaze, didn't he? He has been plotting his revenge down there. And now the time has come. He is creeping towards us, step by step. He is almost at the top."

Lucien's eyes bulged. "He is as monstrous and fierce as a black cloud that has fossilised. And yet his power has not waned. He has communed with the other demons of the deep; he has unchained the terrors of the abyss. Beelzebub is his master and his head is an exposed hollow skull in which lives an evil mouse, bloated on the blood of innocents! His tail is a living serpent and his bristling fur is poisonous to the touch, like solidified toxic fumes. The mould and damp earth of the grave fall from his curved spine in steaming heaps."

Lucien began to drool with terror. "Any moment now, he is going to burst through the cellar door, hissing and spitting. He has turned himself into a gigantic leech or a basilisk. Any moment now..."

The lights came on.

Lucien breathed a sigh of relief. It was common knowledge that electric light, unlike candlelight, was adequate protection against all manner of supernatural bugaboos, be they demons, ghosts or hobgoblins.

A triumphant smile crossed his face. He gazed at Miranda. "Well, I was right, wasn't I? Nothing came out of the cellar door. I have won the bet!"

Miranda shook her head. "You have lost. Something *did* come out of the cellar door. And it *was* very terrible. Awful, even."

"What was it?" Lucien recoiled. Fear gripped him again. He could see his fate reflected in her eyes: a whole month of dusting, cleaning and washing-up.

Nervously, he awaited her answer.

"A story," she said.

Cat on a Unicycle

Meeow meow meow (puff)
meeow hiss meeow meeow hiss
Grrr meeow (pant) meow
meeow meeow meeow meeow meow
Meeow (pedal pedal pedal) hiss
Meeeeeeeeow
Meeow hiss meeow hiss hiss
scowl hiss scowl grrr meow
meeow (gasp) meeow (scratch)
Meeow (puff) meeow hiss (pant)
Hisssssssss
meeow meeow meeow scratch grrr
meeow meeow meeow meeow meow
meeow hiss grrr hiss
meeow hiss meeow (screech!!!)
BUGGER!!!

The Magic Kitten

"Good morning dear!" cried Aunt Emily as she breezed into the study. "And how are you feeling today?"

Michael groaned. He was in no mood for pleasantries. He was seated on an easy chair in front of the French windows, where they had placed him after his legs had been set.

"What have you got there?" he demanded.

"A present for you, dear. Something to cheer you up. I bought it in the market yesterday. What do you think?"

She held up a tiny kitten and put it down on the table next to his chair. It was the most pathetic creature Michael had ever seen.

"I thought it looked lucky," Aunt Emily explained. "It might even work like a magic charm. You never know."

"Very nice." Michael shuddered. He studied the kitten more closely. It was in bad condition. Aunt Emily had always had an eccentric taste in presents. He had never forgotten the coat-hangers she had once bought him for his birthday.

"Anyway, I can't stop." Aunt Emily kissed her nephew on the cheek. "I have to make the jam tarts for the fête this afternoon. It's a pity you won't be able to join us. Nasty things, bicycles."

Michael felt like protesting. After all, Aunt Emily had bought him the bicycle in the first place. He had only tested it out to please her. It had been another unwanted present.

He watched her depart through the open French windows and then sighed. He was now stuck with the kitten. Aunt Emily had placed it just out of reach. He frowned as he remembered what she had said about a magic charm. He was too old for such nonsense. He had recently turned thirty-five, but she still seemed to think of him as a boy.

"Nobody believes in magic anymore!" he muttered to himself. He grimaced as his left foot began to itch. With his legs encased in plaster, it was impossible to scratch his feet. He had to sit still and suffer. Beads of sweat stood out on his forehead.

At least, he thought, things couldn't get any worse.

Looking up through the windows, he gasped in dismay. Ralph Trellis was coming up the path, smiling his usual smug smile.

Of all the villagers, Ralph Trellis annoyed Michael the most. Ralph was a smooth talker who had managed to entice Michael's girlfriend away. Michael still bore a grudge, even though he had avenged himself by spending a whole night outside Ralph's house, shaking his fist and shouting: "Thief! My beautiful girl! You dirty thief!"

Michael scowled and clenched his teeth.

"Now what can *he* want?" he wondered.

"Merely a passing visit," Ralph said as he stepped through the windows. "I'm going to help set up the marquee for the fête. Just thought I'd look in first to see how you are."

"You have a stall this year?" Michael tried to disguise the bitterness in his voice. It was hard work.

"I'm afraid not. I couldn't think of any good money-making schemes this time. I could set up a coconut shy, of course, but then I might have to give prizes away. You know me. I'm always after something for nothing."

"Indeed."

Ralph noticed the kitten. "A new cat, I see."

"It was a present. Do you like it?" A sudden idea struck Michael. He began to see how he could be rid of the ghastly animal and also score a point against Ralph.

"It looks very cute," Ralph said tactfully.

"In that case, as a mark of our friendship, I would like you to have it."

47

"Oh no, I couldn't possibly accept." Ralph was horrified.

"I insist. It's a magic charm." Michael smiled and Ralph had no choice but to take the kitten and offer his thanks. Michael could tell that he was already wondering how best to dispose of the worthless gift. There couldn't possibly be any use for such a tiny mewling beast.

After Ralph had gone, Michael settled down again and chuckled to himself. He had finally outwitted his foe. And now he could look forward to a restful day, at least until the fête was over.

He closed his eyes, enjoying the warmth of the sun on his face, the twittering of the birds in the garden. Before long, he had fallen into a deep sleep.

He was awakened quite roughly. Aunt Emily was standing over him, shaking him by the shoulders.

"Aunt Emily?" He rubbed his bleary eyes. "Is the fête over?"

"Not yet dear. That is why I'm in a rush. You must forgive me, but this is an important matter. You know that kitten I gave you this morning? Well, I want it back."

"Whatever for?"

"A man at the fête has set up a stall. He's got a kitten that works like a magic charm. He's letting people stroke and pat it for a small fee. If the kitten purrs, then you can make a wish and it will come true!"

Michael's jaw dropped open. He gazed at his Aunt in astonishment. His foot started itching again. "Nobody believes in magic anymore!" he protested. "Do they?"

"Of course they do. And the funny thing is that his kitten looks exactly the same as yours. If you give it back to me now, I can set up a rival stall. I've already sold all of my jam tarts."

A sudden fear wrinkled up Michael's brow. "Is he

making a lot of money then, this man?"

"My dear," cried Aunt Emily as she looked around the room, searching for the kitten in question, "he's making an absolute fortune."

That night, Michael insisted that Aunt Emily wheel him out in his chair to Ralph's house where, until dawn unstitched the stars from the velvet sky, he shook his fist and shouted: "Thief! My beautiful cat! You dirty thief!"

Lunar Love Cats

Are *four lines* of poetry enough
for a pair of *felines* in love
with a full time moon above?
That's all I can spare, so tough!

The Pig Iron Mouse Dooms the Moon

I'll tell you why I hate the moon so much, said the Pig Iron Mouse, his whiskers twitching and picking up radio broadcasts from far away. I don't have any secrets, and if I did I wouldn't keep them from my friends, and even if you weren't my friends I would tell you anyway, I would, he added with magnetic sincerity.

The light, that's why, that's the reason! That mellow spreading on the charred toast of the shadowy landscape of night, it makes life harder for any nocturnal creature that fears predators. And I live in constant dread of the Molybdenum Cat, that prowling howling demon with the electric headlamp eyebeams.

He can switch them off when the moon's full and then he's more dangerous than ever and only last year he pounced on the Cupronickel Vole and dented him to death with his teeth, and that's not the way I want to go, no sir, no madam, not the way at all! Pounced on from behind a tumbled stack of science journals.

So I decided to get rid of the moon, do away with it, break the blasted thing and even the odds a little, a smidgen, a sliver. And I thought of ways I might accomplish this feat and it occurred to me that maybe the best course of action would be to catch the moon as it touched the horizon on its way to bed. I decided to impale it.

Now I'm not cruel, not at all, and I didn't want to make the moon suffer, so I raised a very long thin sharp pole on the horizon and I greased it for the entire length, and I knew that the moon's doom would be quick on that slick skewer and nearly painless. I used all my engineering expertise to make that deadly pole, truly I did.

Then I waited for the moon to rise in the east and travel across the sky and settle down unawares on my lethal spike, but for some reason the full fool missed my trap, cunningly wrought and perfectly positioned as it was, and set *behind* the pole. I was dismayed, let me tell you! Had I made an error with my calculations?

Well, I set off on foot and reached the base of the pole and there I saw that it no longer stood on the horizon. Somehow the horizon had moved further away to the west. Maybe it was migrating for the season, heading elsewhere to breed or feed or do whatever it is that horizons do to keep themselves in line, I don't know.

So I made another pole at the place where the horizon had gone to, it was an identical greased spike, long thin sharp, and I waited again and once more the moon missed the point and set behind it. I puffed my cheeks and popped a rivet in the left one, that's how exasperated I was, and I set off to locate the new site of the horizon.

This went on and on and I never succeeded in impaling the moon and one morning I reached the horizon and saw that a pole was already there. It was the first one I had fixed in place. I had gone right around the entire planet! That realisation annoyed me slightly and I felt despondent and very tired and I was embarrassed also.

You are going to ask me where the Molybdenum Cat was during this time. It's a good question and the answer is that I don't know, no sir, no madam, but I guess he was around about, lurking, smirking, metal fur bristling, waiting for the opportunity to pounce, but that opportunity clearly never came, for here I am, still here, me, talking to you.

I wanted to know, continued the Pig Iron Mouse, how the moon was avoiding my traps so successfully, so I decided to find out. What I did was this, he added, his whiskers drooping and the signal fading and the strange dance music from distant lands dying. I plucked out my left eyeball, the one above the cheek that had popped the rivet, I did.

I plucked it out and it was already loose, so it didn't hurt much, and I made a rocket engine powerful enough to carry that eyeball, which after all was a minimal payload, out of our atmosphere, with its odour of buttercups and weasels, and into space, outer space, and through the void, the external void, all the way to the moon, and down.

When the eyeball was safely down on the surface of the moon, it was able to peer up at our planet, the world we're standing on right now, and watch as the Earth travelled across the sky and set on the horizon. That's what it saw, and because it saw that then so did I, because it was my eye, still my eye, up there on the moon, our moon.

And then I realised that it was all a matter of perspective. That's why I had failed to impale the moon! From the surface of the moon things looked very different, very different indeed, yes sir, yes madam, and in fact it was the Earth that was doing the setting on the horizon, not the moon. Which explains why it wasn't landing on my spikes.

Perspective was to blame, that's what I concluded after my eye saw all that, so I decided to approach the problem from that angle. I went to the government department responsible for perspective and I knocked on the front door but it didn't open, so I knocked on it again even harder and it still remained shut, but a window gaped wide.

The window was high up, on the top level of the building, and an unseen voice called down at me, saying: sorry, no member of the public is allowed inside the Department of Perspective, please go away and don't come back! And then the window was closed with a bang and I pretended to go away but in fact I hid and waited for nightfall.

Then I entered the building by climbing onto the roof and sliding down the chimney. Once I was inside I located the room where they keep the machines that control perspective, devices that ensure that parallel lines stretching to infinity only *seem* to converge at a distant point but don't really, and I adjusted the dials more to my liking.

Then I sabotaged those machines so they were stuck like that. And I climbed back out of the chimney and headed for home and now I noticed that the two parallel lines of the railway track I walked down really did meet at a point, and that point was next to my house. I turned my key in the door and it was very late when I went to bed.

When I awoke early in the morning I went to prepare my breakfast and I had broccoli and chocolate as usual, but something had changed. The pieces of broccoli looked like the trees of a rainforest and the triangular wedges of chocolate resembled alpine peaks, and because the laws of perspective had been changed they really were that massive.

Needless to say, I only nibbled at them and then I went out and amused myself by filling my cheeks with air and puffing at distant towers that instantly fell down because they were only as big as they looked, whereas objects that were near my remaining eye seemed large and therefore were. A lost child's marble was like a fallen moon.

When the real moon appeared in the sky, continued the Pig Iron Mouse, I simply reached out and snatched it in my jaws. Then I crunched it to pieces between my teeth. Can't say it was particularly tasty. No sooner had I finished than I spied the Molybdenum Cat far away, coming over the horizon like an idle thought. I seized my chance.

I lunged at his tiny figure and I don't rightly know what happened next but he vanished from sight. I'm fairly sure I didn't swallow him. The only plausible explanation is that he jumped into my empty eye socket, the left one, and hid inside the cave it formed. Probably he still lives there, like something out of prehistory, warming his paws around a fire.

I bet he even invites passing travellers inside to sit around the flames with him while he entertains them with stories, tales about the Pig Iron Mouse, like this one for example, *exactly* like this one in fact, told from the viewpoint of the Pig Iron Mouse himself, just to be clever. And now the flames are dying down and I'll bid you a moonless goodnight.

The Cat that Got the Cream

Tufty was the cat
that got the cream but he went
very far to get it.
Out the door and down the street
on his little furry feet
following the North Star
in a sort of waking dream.

Who had sent this gentle puss
on such an arduous errand?
Naught other than
his own desire to see the world
before he expired
compelled him through the night.
For sure he must get
the cream before it curdled.

He made no fuss
but simply leapt every hurdle
on his lonesome path.
Over walls and hedges he did go
until he reached his
destination, which was the local
train station, and there
he waited for the milk train
to arrive at long last.

Shaken and churned
by the motion of the locomotive
the milk should be
the finest cream he might hope to see
or sniff and taste
in summer, winter or any season.
This at least was Tufty's
reasoning... He wasn't wrong.

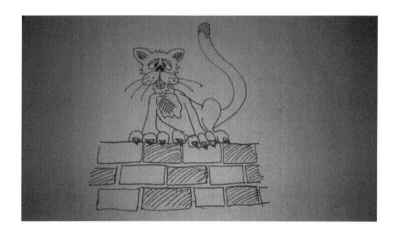

The Big Lick

After all, it was a magnificent house. They could feel no regrets as they received the key from the plump fingers of the estate-agent. A large detached modern dwelling; the house of the future. One kind of future, at any rate. As a light breeze ruffled the fur on the walls, Tony smiled and opened the door. The house purred. They had been accepted.

Inside, they saw that everything was waiting for them exactly as they had arranged. The old battered sofa was there; the one they had bought for their first flat. And the little ornaments from their many travels to exotic lands. And the books and musical instruments scattered over the floor. What more could they ask for? What doubts could they have now? They would be happy here, they would be safe.

Tony turned to Claire and embraced her. "Our new home," he said simply. And then, as if determined to wax lyrical before the wax melted, he added: "Debt where is thy sting? Ground Rent where is thy victory?"

It was essential to satisfy a few outmoded traditions. Tony attempted to carry Claire over the threshold; he grunted but could not obtain sufficient leverage. So it was Claire who carried Tony over, dumping him in a contented heap before the inglenook of the authentic hearth, on an indigo rug all knotted with abstract designs in colours that should have clashed but did not.

They spent the rest of that evening watching the television, snug beyond good taste in each other's company, nibbling shortbread or lobes or upper lips, while some cartoon rodent raced across a landscape as harsh and surreal as any by Dali. The house began to chatter and crouched low, as if ready to spring. With a sudden flash of terrible insight, Tony reached for the remote control and switched channels. Almost at once, the house lost interest.

"It's the mouse," Tony explained, referring to the cartoon. "The house was getting excited. We'll have to be more careful."

Claire nodded vaguely, her mind too frantic with serenity to pay much attention to his words. She had already hung her needlework above the mantelpiece over the grate, and was already planning a sequel. HOME NUTRASWEET HOME would be a project worthy of a six-month energy package, made up of lots of little delicate motions and more thought. The votive lights in her eyes were at once bright and distant.

They had first chanced upon the house while gliding on a picnic quest down the road that led out of the city and into the hills. There it had napped, curled up tight, tail wrapped round the trunk of an old tree that lurched out of mossy ground. They had fallen in love with it immediately; the glistening black fur with the white ruff, the delightful expression and endearing sundries. They had stopped, noticed that it was for sale and had made enquiries.

The estate agent was a large oily man with an absurd hairstyle. Arnie Troppmann had been selling state-of-the-art houses for more than a decade. His experience revealed itself every time he smiled; a gold tooth encrusted with diamonds. He mopped his forehead with a contract, shook rancid buttery hands and showed them around the building, pointing out features with an enthusiasm that was not only infectious but positively septic.

"These latest models are self-regulating. They have a nervous system based on that of the domesticated cat. As you can see, the fur covers the inside walls as well as the whole exterior, minimizing heat loss. The house is extremely sensitive to outside changes and will warn you of the approach of intruders or rain. It has a superb sense of balance guaranteed to withstand the most violent earthquakes. Also it is self-cleaning. Every Monday night."

And now as Claire and Tony blinked in surprise, two enormous eyes appeared on the ceiling from nowhere, flooding the room with soft yellow light. This was another fixture designed for the conservation of energy: reflected starlight amplified and focused wherever it was needed most. The house, they also quickly discovered, had a wonderful sense of smell and hearing. The rose garden seemed constantly within, rather than without, the enclosed lounge and the music of the wind playing the kazoo on separate blades of grass charmed them to sleep with Aeolian lullabies.

The following evening, at roughly the same time, the fur on the walls pricked up alarmingly and the house arched its roof. Tony and Claire were instantly aware that trouble was afoot. Bounding into the kitchen, Tony snatched a garlic crusher and bore it to the front door, which he threw open with a flourish, at the same instant daring any intruder to approach closer. He was startled by a mangy hound which, though no clove, was sufficiently impressed by the unlikely weapon to beat a hasty retreat.

"Scat!" cried Tony, which was both completely unnecessary and unnecessarily complete. He pumped the garlic crusher handle a few times in sullen victory. "A stray," he explained to Claire. "An unkempt mutt. Reminded me a little of Toasted Muffin." And he fell into a redundant fugue, a nostalgic slice from the melon of his youth: his dog, his air rifle, the heel of a loaf, the nettle-itch and the doc-leaf wrap. Toasted Muffin, he recalled, had been run over by a tractor.

On Monday night, they decided to stay indoors yet again. It was cleaning night, after all. The estate agent had warned them to absent themselves at this time, but they were too curious to see what would happen. Besides, Troppmann had also suggested that if any problems arose they should come to see him and he would put matters right. So there was nothing to worry about. They waited for the show to begin. They waited and watched.

Thus it was that when Troppmann himself was pulled out of bed in the early hours, cursing and sweating, to answer the door, he knew that it would soon be time to start breaking promises. But at first he did not recognise the raw-red couple who leered through the glass door at him and he refused to let them in. They seemed to be covered in some sticky substance and they pounded on the door with a disturbing sort of squelch.

"Please may we have our skins back?"

The Mice Will Play

"The cat is late," announced Mark.

But Vanessa shook her head. "The cat has a name."

"*Pangur Bán*," hissed Mark.

"Well?" murmured Vanessa with hooded eyes.

"Our dear friend Pangur Bán is late. Is that better? He's not here. He is absent. We remain unmolested."

It was true. They lay next to each other in bed under an unoccupied quilt. He was not sitting on it, kneading the pattern of interlocking squares, snagging an occasional claw on a loose thread, glaring at them with large yellow eyes. There was no presence demanding breakfast. They were free to drift back to sleep, and yet it was already an hour past dawn. The situation was unprecedented.

"What if he's ill?" cried Vanessa.

Mark sighed and his knees twitched, as if he really intended to get up and go down. "I'll take a look..."

Vanessa decided to treat this as a genuine offer. "Good idea."

"Shall I bring you a cup of tea as well?"

She smiled. "Yes please."

He scowled and stood and struggled to pull on his trousers. From Vanessa's position, it looked as if he was trying to escape a quicksand.

Pangur Bán was gone. There could be no more doubt about it. Mark brought the news up the stairs with the tea. Vanessa sampled both with a pout. Then she said:

"Go out into the garden and call for him."

Mark blushed. "Why should I?"

"It's your moral duty."

He hunched his shoulders and stepped towards the

window. He always felt embarrassed calling a cat's name in public. The neighbours might hear. It didn't seem a very manly thing to do: he couldn't say why. He looked down onto the garden. There was movement in the bushes, a flash of dark caramel, like toasted sunlight.

"A cat!" he squealed.

Vanessa was by his side. "Where?"

"Cover yourself!" he spluttered. "The neighbours..."

"Pangur Bán?"

"No."

"A different cat? In our garden?"

He frowned. "I'd say so."

They went down together, she wrapped in a dressing gown with a frayed belt. This was destined to snap and expose her excellent bosom to the world. Mark knew that. He continued to frown, lacking the incentive to do anything else with his face. The cat flap was still swinging and muddy pawprints outlined a complex dance on the stone tiles. He stood above them as if he was decoding a choreography diagram. At the furthest limit of the prints lay a mouse, very dead.

"A present for us," he said.

"The alien cat must have brought it," he added later, over coffee. "For us to eat. Our breakfast on this fine morning."

"But I'm a vegetarian," sniffed Vanessa.

"A concept beyond a cat's understanding..."

"I want Pangur Bán back."

"You do indeed," he conceded ruefully.

They chewed toast in silence. The mouse had been quietly disposed of. The absence of Pangur Bán was dramatic, like the simmering aftermath of an argument when all words have been exhausted but rage still twists the heart into a corkscrew. The morning was ruined. Already Mark felt the rest of the day weighing on him, interminable, awful. And there was no escape, nowhere to go. It was Sunday.

"I might put up those shelves later," he suggested.

"No you won't."

"Or fix your portable steam-cleaner."

"Not that."

He threw down his knife into the jam pot. It did not stick deep and quiver upright as he had hoped. It was not the strike of a hero. It penetrated half an inch and overbalanced, staining the tablecloth a pale cherry.

"What then?" he demanded, slamming his fist, but the cups did not rattle.

She raised her eyebrows at his uselessness and said: "You will call Pangur Bán until he comes. And if he does not come, you must call him some more."

"Yes," he mumbled with lowered head.

Vanessa sat in her rocking chair and thought about her cat and his huffs. He was big on huffs and good at them. When he wanted milk and there was none to be had, or when his favourite windowsill was cluttered with ornaments, or when he burned his nose on a candle: at these times and others he would demonstrate his ability at the art of huffing. His back turned to the object of dismay, his tail lashing like an electric cable severed in a storm, he would emit a constant low note, not quite a growl, not quite a squeak, but a complex tone pitched somewhere between the two, like bagpipes sat on by a hungry man.

His big huffs were noteworthy, but his biggest huff was incredible. He indulged it once a year. Whenever they went off on holiday, they would make arrangements for a friend to visit the house and feed him. Pangur Bán was very precise in his dietary requirements, which included the angle of his bowl in relation to his milk dish. A lapse in this respect was most irksome to him. However hard the friends tried, they made mistakes. Pangur Bán would use bristling scowls to teach them what was wrong, and slowly over the course of the week they would make enough little adjustments to satisfy his feline majesty. By this time, Mark and Vanessa would be back, and the biggest huff would be discharged in their direction. It was an annual event.

Now Vanessa craned her head at weird noises which were emerging from the adjacent room. She rose and wandered in their direction. She stood on the threshold of the open door.

"What are you doing?" she demanded.

Mark lowered the handkerchief from his mouth. "Recording my voice."

She realised he had been talking into a microphone. "Why?"

"To call the cat. I'm going to make a tape-loop of me calling his name over and over. And then I can play it outside and call him all day without tiring, and still have time to do other things."

"But why the handkerchief?"

He licked his lips anxiously. "So the neighbours won't think it's me."

Pangur Bán did not come back, but the strange cat did. They caught sight of its tail disappearing through the cat flap. And there was another mouse, but this time the cupboards were open and the plates were strewn about the floor around it. A very distasteful sight.

"The little rascal!" muttered Mark.

"Rummaging among our things!" growled Vanessa.

"Where does it come from, I wonder?"

Vanessa stooped to pick up the mouse by the tail. Mark was left to clear up the plates.

63

"Pangur Bán! Pangur Bán!" called a voice from the garden.

"It's going to rain," said Vanessa.

"I'll bring the tape recorder inside," replied Mark.

"That's for the best."

Mark went out and Vanessa seemed to hear the giggles of neighbours. Probably a trick of the wind in the bushes. The weather was taking a turn for the worse. And Pangur Bán was exposed to the elements. So was her husband, but he didn't count as much.

"Poor thing!" she said when he returned.

"Thank you," responded Mark, but then he realised she was looking beyond him into the garden. He sighed. "I wish I was a cat!"

She regarded him with surprise.

"You're *full* of good ideas today!" she exclaimed.

The sun went down and stayed there, but they went the other way, up to bed. The early stars twinkled through the window over the roofs of houses. Two of them were yellow.

"Like Pangur Bán's eyes," Vanessa remarked.

"You don't think he has become a constellation?"

"Don't be silly!" she chided.

He accepted the rebuke mildly, for he was her husband. "You know something? He would never have allowed us to retire to bed at this hour, if he was still here. He always had his supper at midnight."

"What are you saying?"

"That maybe the absence of Pangur Bán has a few advantages."

"Such as?"

He swallowed dryly. "We are free to play."

"In what way?"

"Well, we can read books or make love. We can do

these things in peace!"

She was silent for a whole minute.

"Shall we try both of them? Now?" she asked.

"In any particular order? Or at the same time?"

"Silly!" she repeated, but now she meant it as a compliment.

There was a third mouse waiting for them when they went down the next morning. And the cupboards were open again. But now some effort had been made to drag the plates to the table. They had been abandoned under that item of furniture. Mark and Vanessa tidied them up together, more at ease in each other's company than they had been for years.

"What does this mean?" they wondered.

There was no sensible answer. But the clock was urging them to work, chopping the riddle to pieces with every jolt of its rapier-thin second hand. As they rushed coffee and prepared to leave, Mark indicated the cat flap with a nod of his head.

"Shall I lock it?"

"To stop the strange cat getting in? But what about Pangur Bán?"

He shrugged. "Fair enough."

"Leave it open..."

He frowned as they passed through the hallway and reached the front door. "Do you think it really is trying to *look after* us?"

"The new cat?"

"Leaving food, I mean. Nearly laying the table..."

She smiled without irony. "If it wants to do the washing and ironing too, I don't mind!"

"Better make the most of it."

"You're right. How long can this last for?"

*

All week. The alien cat must have entered the house twice every day. The evidence was there when Mark and Vanessa woke in the mornings and when they returned from work in the late afternoons. They caught occasional glimpses of their visitor when they peered through the back windows into the garden. But Pangur Bán himself did not appear.

The ritual with the plates became more uncanny. At last they were forced to the conclusion that the disruption of their kitchen was more serious than a game. There were no more mice. The benefactor was clearly intent on experimenting with a variety of offerings. A blackbird, a goldfish and a chicken leg undoubtedly raided from some dustbin: these were prepared just for them with feline elegance, dumped in the middle of plates and ungarnished.

Cutlery soon joined the crockery. Forks, knives and a spoon, positioned around the plates. Then the salt and pepper. Empty glasses were added on Thursday. An extraordinary achievement for a cat to manipulate such objects with its paws! Vanessa began to perceive a curious symmetry in this behaviour.

"I think I know where Pangur Bán is," she said on the final morning of the working week.

Mark gasped. "Where?"

"On holiday."

"What?" he blurted.

"Probably abroad. He's copying us. Every year we go away and arrange for a friend to feed him. He has done the same."

"Don't be absurd!"

"Consider more carefully. It makes perfect sense. If Pangur Bán's meals aren't arranged properly, he refuses to eat. And that's what we've been doing: refusing to eat! So the other cat has been adjusting its offerings to us and also the manner of presentation."

"What an idea! It's ridiculous," he shouted. Then he added more thoughtfully: "So yes, I guess it might be true..."

At the end of the day she found him standing at their front door. She gripped his elbow. "What's wrong?"

"I was waiting for you."

"Why?" she asked.

"I don't want to go in alone."

"But you finish work an hour before me!" she cried.

"Yes, I've been loitering here. I have a feeling something grand is about to happen when we step inside."

She wrinkled her nose. "What's that smell?"

"I think it's basil and walnut tagliatelle."

She pressed her ear to the door. "I can hear pots and pans being rattled. And now a cork popping."

They held each other very close.

"Let's open the door," she said at last.

There was a single candle on the table. The flame flickered in the gentle gust from the swinging cat flap.

The two glasses were filled with wine.

Mark sat and tucked the napkin into his shirt. After a moment's hesitation, Vanessa followed his example.

They broke freshly-baked bread.

"This meal is truly wonderful!" he exclaimed.

Vanessa paused and lowered her fork. "Why didn't we think to check Pangur Bán's basket?"

"What for?"

She rose and moved to the corner of the room, grasping the basket and holding it upside-down. The blankets fell out, and underneath them a selection of glossy magazines and pamphlets.

"What are these?" he cried.

She examined them. "Holiday brochures."

"Where for?"

"Catalonia!" she laughed. "Where else?"

The following morning they were woken by the postman sliding the mail under the door. They raced down to seize it. Among the bills and promotional offers, there was a single postcard.

"Barcelona!" panted Vanessa.

"What does it say?" gulped Mark, trying to read over her shoulder.

She inspected it. "I don't know!"

"Perhaps he can't write English?"

She nodded sagely. "He's a cat."

"In that case, how did the postman decipher the address?"

They exchanged profound glances. Then they opened the door and ran out onto the pavement. The postman was already at the end of the street. But this was the moment Mark had been waiting for, half in dread, half in hope. The belt of her dressing-gown finally snapped. He covered her excellent bosom with his hands and helped her back inside. No point causing a public disturbance.

"Shall we meet him at the airport?" she asked.

He shook his head. "Cats probably have other methods of leaving the country. Pea-green boats and suchlike."

"I hope he has bought us a nice souvenir."

"Same here."

"What shall we do now?"

They licked their lips and said together: "When the cat's away..."

Absolutely.

Cats' Eyes

We were on the right road. The presence of cats' eyes told us that nothing had gone amiss, that no errors of navigation had been made. In the darkness of a remote rural region during a moonless night it was a comfort to know that this line of glass studs would reflect our headlights and be a most reliable guide to our ultimate destination.

But something went wrong anyway. It was hard to explain why this should be so and I suspect I would decline the opportunity to know the reasons even if they were available. We must have taken an unintentional turning somewhere along our route. I said, "The cats' eyes have gone," and she nodded in the gloom and answered, "Dogs' ears."

It was true. This new road clearly had different rules to the old. The reflective glass studs had been replaced by flexible triangles that echoed every sound our vehicle made, including the conversations we held inside it, and threw the audio signals back at us, horribly amplified. "Turn off at the next junction," I advised and she did so.

But this new road was even stranger and more disturbing and certainly of less practical use. Lips puckered at us and we tasted afresh the meals we had lately eaten. "Weasels' mouths," she said, her frown so deep that it changed the outline of her face in profile when I glanced at her. We found another road and became more than hopelessly lost.

My nostrils were flooded with the bittersweet aromas of nostalgia, the pangs like vanilla, the regrets a new kind of smelling salts. "Aardvarks' noses! Who builds these roads?" I muttered. Every muscle in my body was tense. She maintained a steady speed but we both knew that morning would never appear in time. We took another detour.

This road was the most harrowing of all. Have you ever driven along a narrow country lane festooned with lemurs' fingers? It is a tricky and ticklish challenge. We laugh in despair while the men who invent these things sit alone in uncarpeted mansions, a dead television in every room, counting and recounting their own senses.

Alphabeticat

Following the letter **C**
He saw the letter **A**
Invited them both for **T**
It was such a purrfect day!

A Word in Your Shell-Like

Hope was a tortoiseshell cat and Hopkins, who had named her, often wondered about this. He thought it was unfair. Who, he asked himself, had loved tortoises so much that they had decided to compare the colour of a certain type of feline to the hard covering of the reptile?

After all, no one ever describes a tortoise as a 'cat-fur tortoise' and no one ever would. It simply doesn't work the other way around, thought Hopkins with a frown as he stroked Hope under the chin.

Hope purred but she was a little bored with his egotism.

It seemed extreme even to her.

Hopkins loved himself more than anything else and he never allowed any chance to demonstrate this love to slip through his slim fingers. Giving his cat a name based on his own was the least of it. There were mirrors on every wall and he constantly moved among endless illusory corridors full of his reflected image, an infinite glassy maze of himself.

But Hope didn't really enjoy seeing herself everywhere. She put up with it because it was easier than leaving and finding a new home. She would do that if it became necessary, of course, but it wasn't quite necessary yet. Hopkins hadn't gone too far, though he was close.

He had just returned from a weekend at the seaside. He had gone to relax in the town of Tenby in Wales. It is everything a seaside resort should be and he had enjoyed himself in a quiet way, but now he was back and eager to show off his acquisitions. To be more accurate: his acquisition, singular. He had found an enormous lovely shell on the beach.

Not the shell of a tortoise. That needs to cleared up right away. No, it was the shell of some sea creature that had lived a secret life in the depths of the blue and finally had washed up onto land.

"Look Hope!" he crooned as he held it up.

It caught the light of the early morning sun that poked its beams under the curtain that failed to fully cover a window in the same way that a man might, for unknown but possibly dubious reasons, poke his fingers through a letterflap. The shell gleamed, glinted and coruscated with colour. Then Hopkins held it close to his ear and listened for several minutes.

"I can hear the sea," he said with immense satisfaction.

Hope continued to purr softly.

"That's the thing about shells, especially big examples like this. You can hear the sea in them, the sea where they lived. If you can get your ear inside you can almost feel the splashing of the briny water. I am listening to the waves now and they are rustling pebbles on a shore."

Hope flicked her tail twice against the polished surface of the desk with a dull drumming sound. They were in the study, the room where Hopkins kept all the mementoes and souvenirs of his travels and trips. All of them reminded him more of himself than of the places they had come from. That was the point. This shell was no different. He lowered it.

"I heard the very beach where I found it," he said.

Hope didn't respond in any way.

"It's true," insisted Hopkins, lifting the shell to his other ear. "I recognise the pulse of the waves, the rhythm of the incoming tide, like the purring of some contented beast. And guess what? Guess!"

Hope licked a paw instead of guessing, but Hopkins shook his head. "No, you won't be able to get the answer. It's too inexplicable. But I can hear *myself* on that beach, walking along and stooping down to pick up the shell, the shell I am listening to right now. Imagine that!"

A grin broke open the lower half of his face.

"I can even hear myself exclaiming at the beauty of the shell and talking to myself, muttering about how wonderful it is. 'I am going to take this home,' I am saying, 'and one day I will hold it up to my ear and listen and hear myself walking along this beach and finding it. I will hear *this* moment and I will even hear myself saying these words right now'. How amazing is that? I predicted the outcome and I was absolutely correct!"

Hope was less than impressed. To her it seemed a self-fulfilling prophecy rather than a genuine act of deduction or clairvoyance. But Hopkins had the look of a lunatic, the same sort of expression as that person must have had, whoever he or she was, who first compared cats to tortoises. Maybe it was Achilles, more likely it wasn't. He lowered the shell again.

It stood on the desk like a suit of armour for a dream.

"What do you think now?"

Hopkins was leaning forward and questioning her.

"Don't you agree that your master is the cleverest fellow you have met? I constantly astound myself, truly I do!"

Hope closed her eyes and pretended to slumber.

Hopkins chuckled to himself.

Then he went away, leaving the study with that shuffling gait of his in the slippers he had commissioned to be made with little mirrors sewn to the tops of the toes. When he peered down he saw himself peering up. And when he peered up, mirrors in the ceiling showed himself peering down. Peering down at himself in the slippers peering up at himself.

It could have been overwhelmingly confusing.

But not for Hopkins. For him it was the simplest and purest love of all. It couldn't be long now before he asked himself for his own hand in marriage and it was almost certain he would say yes.

Hope opened her eyes again. The shell was there.

She glanced around. The study was a tangle of shadows and sunbeams. A problem with hanging mirrors everywhere was that sunlight tended to bounce all over the house if it was allowed in, glaring and blinding and scorching wallpaper and melting plastic ornaments. And this was why Hopkins generally kept all the curtains drawn, but he couldn't keep out every single beam and it only took one stray ray to knit itself a cat's cradle of light upstairs and downstairs and in every room and corner. Cat's cradle, thought Hope.

She stood and stretched. Then she yawned wide.

Then she approached the shell.

It really was large, bigger than her. What sort of monster must have lived in it once? Something with tentacles, with sad undersea eyes, with suckers and a beak and fins! Who knew? Not Hope.

She stepped closer, softly, and now she thought she could hear something issuing from the mouth of the shell.

A susurration, a sigh, a yearning and compelling hiss.

The sounds of the sea!

Hope felt the hairs on her back stiffen.

Water, endless water, water as broad as a thousand back gardens, a dread expanse of wetness, of cold misery.

But there was something else, something good.

A word. A solitary word.

And the sound of this word drew her yet closer and the sound of this word was the thing itself, was a splash, a flash.

She poked her head into the mouth of the shell.

The word was louder here, an echo, a web of sound that caught her, drew her in yet deeper, and so she entered the shell. The corridor spiralled inward and it was smooth and shiny and the surface was like a dull mirror, like the passages in the house of Hopkins but nicer too.

The tip of her tail disappeared inside the shell.

And this was the moment when Hopkins returned to the study. He noticed that the cat was gone but thought nothing of it. He picked up the shell, held it to his ear again and listened. And frowned.

He heard himself and his mouth curled at the memory.

The word that had enticed Hope into the dangerous crossing from present to past was a simple one. It was 'fish'.

She emerged from the shell onto a beach.

A man was approaching her.

He stooped and gave her a stroke. "How odd! I have a cat at home that is just like you! A tortoiseshell. Identical!"

Hope allowed herself to be stroked and then she hastened on, making for the town ahead, for her brand new life.

Behind her, the man had found the shell. He had picked it up and he was talking to himself. Hope heard the words.

"I am going to take this home," he was saying decisively, "and one day I will hold it up to my ear and listen and hear myself walking along this beach and finding it. I will hear *this* moment," he added thoughtfully, "and I will even hear myself saying these words right now..."

A tortoiseshell cloud drifted in front of the sun.

Bangers the Mash

Bangers the Mash was a sausage dog. He was very long at the start of this story and he will grow much longer as it proceeds, but this isn't a tall tale because he never learned to stand just on his back legs.

So we have now established that there was once a dog called Bangers the Mash and that he was a sausage dog. You might be asking yourself what a story about a dog is doing in a book of cat tales?

I can't answer that because the question depends on whether this story really has appeared in a book of cat tales or not and I'm simply unable to know that. You see, I am writing this story *before* it is published, which is the only proper way to write original fiction.

It might never appear in any sort of book at all.

That's always a possibility.

But if forced to give an answer, I would say something along the lines of how breaking up a general theme with a story that doesn't fit helps to refresh that theme. Alternatively I might declare that perhaps there are cats in this story after all but we haven't got to them yet.

Bangers the Mash was a sausage dog.

Let's not forget that fact.

He ended up the longest sausage dog that ever was.

He was about *this* long when his owner acquired him and within a year he grew to be *that* long, which is long but not too long. His owner was named Sally and she devoted much of her spare time to her allotment. She took her dog with her whenever she went to work on it.

He was known just as Bangers at first.

His surname was earned in a most amusing and peculiar manner. One day while they were on her plot of land there was an unexpected and ferocious storm and Sally and Bangers took refuge in her shed and waited for everything to calm down. It rained and rained and rained and there was thunder and lightning. Then a bolt of bright blue electricity struck the earth where she was growing potatoes and the ground trembled and steamed.

The blast had stripped away the soil and exposed the potatoes and they were baked, all of them, as if they had been in a fire for a couple of hours. Something happened to Bangers, some primal urge overcame him, and he ran into the rain with his tongue hanging out and began trampling the potatoes. The crispy skins split, the white floury interiors revealed themselves and the dog turned them into mash, into an entire plot of sky-baked spuds.

Thereafter he became 'The Mash' as well as Bangers.

In a not dissimilar way, Sally's previous dog, Vlad the Impala, earned his surname when it turned out he was actually an African antelope. But we are not here today to discuss such exotic creatures.

Bangers the Mash was a sausage dog.

I know I keep repeating myself but it's an important point.

"You've grown longer overnight!"

That was Sally exclaiming with surprise one morning when Bangers came up the stairs and into her bedroom to greet her.

He rarely or never brought her breakfast in bed but that's hardly surprising because he was a dog and dogs don't do that.

"In fact you seem almost to have doubled in length!"

True. But how was this possible?

The fact is that Bangers the Mash had accomplished the amazing feat by a supreme act of determination. He had mentally *willed* himself to stretch longer and longer overnight and so he had.

Sally shook her head, jumped out of bed and dressed quickly. She found a tape measure and used it to determine the exact length of Bangers the Mash. He was two metres long. "Remarkable!"

Then she went down for breakfast. She never ate sausages in front of him. It seemed cruel. She munched muesli instead.

"I wonder what's on the radio today?" she asked.

She pushed her bowl aside.

Then she walked over to the radio on the mantelpiece.

"Just an old sock," she said.

There was always an old sock on the radio. It had been flung there years before by Vlad. Sally sighed and asked:

"What shall we do today?"

But Bangers had already decided what *he* was going to do. Grow longer. When she turned to look at him, he was four metres long. Sally frowned. Did this mean he was a bad dog or not?

"Well, I'm keeping my length the length it is," said Sally. "But you can do whatever you like," she added.

Bangers promptly doubled his length again.

He found the trick easy now.

"You are longer than the kitchen," Sally pointed out. And he was. His rear half was in another room entirely.

Sally went out to buy a newspaper. She assumed that when she got back home Bangers would have reverted to his previous size, but that isn't what he'd done. On the contrary, he had doubled his length and doubled it again and now he was thirty-two metres long. His back end up was up the stairs with a twist on the landing and into the spare room. His front end was in the garden. She sighed as she tripped over his brown body.

"Maybe you find this new game amusing, but it's inconvenient for me. I suggest you stop growing physically and grow up emotionally instead. A mature and responsible sausage dog wouldn't annoy me in this fashion. 'Bad Manners Bangers' will be your next name!"

But a process had been set in motion that couldn't be halted. Even if he had wanted to stop growing, Bangers the Mash wasn't sure he'd be able to. The inexorable elongation of his body seemed to accelerate rather than slow as if it were being compelled by a cosmic force.

He concentrated on stretching longer and longer.

Sally left the house again later, this time in order to visit a friend. You might be wondering why she doesn't go to work and how if she doesn't work she earns enough money to pay the mortgage on such a nice house, but this is a short story and you ought to know that characters in fiction have an easier time of things than you do out there in reality.

In her absence, Bangers doubled his length and doubled it again, again, again, again and yet again. Then he tripled it and quadrupled it. He tripled it no less than three times and quadrupled it no less than four. Then he doubled it a few more times. For good measure he doubled it. Sally didn't have to leave the house of her friend in order to see him.

She watched his head move past the window. This house was on the far side of town from Sally's own home.

She jumped up and rushed out. "What are you doing here?" But then she realised he wasn't here, or rather that only part of him was and that some of him was still in her house. So she couldn't tell him off for wandering. She decided to follow him on her bicycle, the same bicycle that she had used to visit her friend, even though I didn't mention it earlier.

I could go back a few paragraphs and do a rewrite, specifying that Sally went on a bicycle to visit her friend, it's still not too late for me to do that, but I won't. It's better to leave things as they are. The important point, the only thing that really matters here, is that Bangers the Mash was getting longer. His body threaded itself down every single street in the town and he was already halfway to the next town. Sally pedalled furiously.

"What are you up to?" she panted when she finally caught up with him, but he promptly doubled himself and was suddenly gone. She stood no chance of matching his velocity and talking just to a body was pointless, so she went home and ate one hundred jam tarts instead.

Why not? It's what I would do.

The days passed, the weeks passed, the months passed and even a year or two passed. Bangers the Mash had now lengthened himself to such an extent he occupied every road and street in the land. There wasn't a single thoroughfare where his body couldn't be found. He was the longest sausage dog ever to exist in the entire history of sausage dogs!

I promised you earlier that this would happen, didn't I, and now I have delivered. Bangers the Mash resembled an elevated walkway that matched the streets below, so that every street seemed to be double stacked, and the reason he had done this to himself? Let me tell you.

It was for the sake of cats.

Yes. Believe it or not, Bangers loved cats

No, he hadn't turned himself into a hairy catwalk for cats, though a few utilised him for this purpose. He had constructed a roof so that cats might walk the streets in the rain without getting wet. The cats were supposed to walk under him. Theoretically they could go anywhere they liked because his body covered all the available geographical options.

Unfortunately his legs were very short.

So the arcade he had turned himself into wasn't very high.

Only kittens and mice used it.

It was a supreme act of misguided altruism by a sausage dog who had probably had his brains scrambled on the night of the storm in the allotment. Still, it's the thought that counts and—

Someone is tugging at my sleeve. It is Sally.

She has approached on her bicycle and I didn't hear her coming. I think she wants me to stop writing this story now. It turns her dog into a figure of fun and he's not really that. She is enticing me away with freshly baked jam tarts. I can't resist. I am going... going... gone...

But Bangers the Mash is still a sausage dog.

The Rescue

"Mayday! Mayday!" hooted the owl
    as the pea-green boat began to sink.
"We're low on honey and plenty of money
    won't serve for a life-raft, I think!
The pussy cat can't swim and even I won't
    be able to flap as far as the shore.
We're in the drink of an appalling bay
    and drowning seems the only way
    that this unfunny day
        is going to finish at all."

"Don't panic," said the confident voice
    over the crackling radio static.
"The Royal National Lifeboat Institutional Society for
the Protection of Talking Fictional Animals
    is coming to you without delay."
    And so it was.

When Pushkin Came to Shovekin

They were moving from the town of Small Mercies to the equally small town of Denial and they were in a mighty rush. The reason they were in such a rush was because rushing is more appropriate on the day of a house move than sitting in soft chairs calmly sipping sweet tea.

More appropriate and more *stylish*, it must be admitted.

Dust and clattering arose everywhere.

Bethan paused for a moment, stood with hands on her hips and her chest heaving in the hallway. Her chest might have been heaving in the hallway but the rest of her was in the lounge, which indicates how generous her bosom was. But this isn't that kind of story, so forget such details and just be aware that she was angry. "Where is the removal truck?"

"For what time did you order it?" came the meek voice of Tommaso, her mate, who was packing his feather dusters.

"I didn't order it for any time at all. *You* were the one who was supposed to order it. That was your task, not mine."

"Ah, I see. You'll have to forgive me but—"

"Forgive you?" Bethan extended her long and powerful arms and began rotating them at high speed from the elbows, as if they were mechanical flails on a collectivised farm. She always did this when she was exasperated but she didn't know why. Nobody would ever know.

"I will order one now."

"Better late than never, I suppose?"

"Yes, that's a good attitude. I will just finish with this pile of red dusters before moving onto the blue ones and—"

"Save yourself the trouble!" snarled Bethan.

She turned and strode to the telephone on the little table, picked it up and dialled the number of a reliable removal company that she had used before. An impressively deep voice answered her.

"How may we assist you? You wish to hire one of our trucks? State your name and town of residence clearly."

"Bethan K. Fullfor, Small Mercies."

"Well, I generally am."

Bethan winced, having heard that joke too often.

More information was exchanged.

"We will be there as soon as humanly possible."

"Only humanly?" said Bethan.

The voice didn't bother answering that one. It had a busy day ahead of it, that voice, and could indulge banter only in short bursts. Bethan replaced the receiver and turned to confront Tommaso. She snatched one of the red dusters out of his hands and slapped him with it.

"You worthless dolt! Take this and that and this again!"

Ten minutes later she desisted.

He was bruised but there wasn't a speck of dust on him.

The truck arrived one hour later.

Bethan threw open the door and allowed the two muscular men standing on the threshold to enter and begin carrying the stuff in relays out of the house and into the back of the truck. Tommaso was the last item to be packed. One of the men lifted him up, held him horizontally under an arm and stowed him with the furniture, ornaments and carpet rolls.

Bethan rode in the front of the truck between the two men, one hand on the left thigh of the right one and the other on the right thigh of the wrong one. The vehicle bounced down the potholed road and her hands sometimes slipped up the legs they rested on. But nobody complained.

83

Tommaso could be heard somewhere far away in the back of the truck. It seemed he was singing or whimpering.

"He doesn't like the dark," explained Bethan.

"Maybe he should ride up here then?" the driver suggested.

"Oh no," she said. "The fact he doesn't like the dark is the reason I put him in the back in the first place. I'm not a nice person, but that doesn't much matter because I have wonderful hair."

"You do indeed. It's very curly," said the men.

"Yes and auburn," agreed Bethan.

That settled the matter. They trundled out of Small Mercies and into the country and down numerous lanes that were only just wide enough for them. It was lucky that nothing came the other way.

The sun was setting when they finally arrived in Denial.

The new house greeted them and it was an empty shell but the men soon filled it with the objects in the back of the truck, including Tommaso, who was shaken but not fatally, and who helped with the rest of the unloading to the best of his limited ability. Then the task was done.

Bethan ostentatiously kissed both of the men farewell.

"Go on, it's your turn!" she said.

"But really, I don't know if I should," spluttered Tommaso.

"You'd better!" she rumbled.

So Tommaso stood on tiptoes and kissed the men too.

"On the lips, you idiot!" cried Bethan.

He didn't dare disobey. The men got back into the truck and drove off in low gear, wiping their mouths with their grubby sleeves and feeling grateful for the dirt that coats the cotton shirts of working men. Not that Tommaso was the worst kisser in the world, just that his tongue had been fluffy, as if he'd bitten a feather duster to mad pieces in captivity.

Bethan watched them depart, then she explored her new home. "Exactly the same size as our last house and the view through the windows is similar. It almost feels as if we haven't moved at all."

"Something's missing," ventured Tommaso.

Bethan narrowed her eyes and her eyebrows stood erect, each hair like a poisoned quill on the back of a specially prepared porcupine. "Oh yes? So you don't like it? Think it lacks character?"

"Not that, not that at all! I meant it literally. Something *is* missing. It's not the telescope or the gramophone or the pianola, nor is it the spittoon or drest of chaws (I'll be perfectly honest and confess that I still don't know what a drest of chaws *is*) or the solar-powered kettle or the hatstand that can hold hats from any period in history, or the clothes horse."

Bethan rubbed her chin. "So what can it be?"

"Don't you have a hunch?"

"No, but I will."

It was the cat. These things are easily done. Cats get left behind just as often, or more frequently perhaps, than dogs, rabbits, canaries and goldfish. Pushkin had been sleeping in the garden during the move.

When he awoke, he stretched his paws and body, yawned wider than the cave of a mouse, padded to the back door and pushed through the cat-flap that always swung open with an astonished squeak.

The house was empty. Pushkin blinked and went wandering through the rooms. As far as he was concerned some disaster must have forced Bethan and Tommaso to flee.

85

He couldn't imagine that anyone would move for such feeble reasons as a new job, which actually is why Bethan *had* changed towns. No, it had to be for something more visceral than that.

Maybe a bear had entered the house and chased them out.

But if so, where was the bear now?

And what was a bear anyway? Pushkin had never seen one.

He searched for food, found none.

"The bear, whatever one is, must have eaten it all," he decided, "and also taken all the furniture, so there's no option for me left but to find my owners. I will have to embark on a hazardous journey. I had better prepare myself for such an epic voyage in the traditional way."

And he licked himself six times in six ritual places.

"I'm ready now," he told himself.

It was getting dark, which was the perfect time to be setting off, so with scarcely a glance behind him, Pushkin returned to the garden through the noisy cat-flap and weaved silently between clumps of long grass on the badly tended lawn all the way to the crumbling brick wall that formed the garden's boundary and then he leaped onto this and over it.

He landed in a foreign garden and was instantly on the alert, for cats that weren't him, namely other cats, owned this territory, or rather they claimed it as part of their own kingdoms, whereas it fact it overlapped with his own and with others. It was on the margins of the civilised world and needed regular patrolling to prevent incursions from rivals, but he didn't have time for that now. He had to keep going in a highly unnatural straight line.

Pushkin distrusted straight lines. They seemed awkward.

Sometimes straight lines were necessary and useful and even essential, as in the top of a garden wall that one wished to use as a path. But Pushkin's quest now would take him over such walls, not along them. He felt an insistent pull in one direction only and decided to keep going that way. His whiskers twitched in rhythm to the undulations of his agile body.

He crossed a dozen gardens and then cleared the last wall into an alley. It was extremely dark here and the way was obstructed with abandoned objects of inconceivable function and it was not an easy matter even for an experienced cat to negotiate the full length of the way. But Pushkin managed it. It disgorged him into a meadow on the edge of Small Mercies.

He had escaped the town. But how far did he have to go?

The countryside was a place that was both enthralling and frightening. He heard the bark of foxes in a nearby wood, the flap of wings that might have been those of hungry owls, the slither of snakes.

But at the end of the day, and the day really *was* over, he was Pushkin, an indefatigable sort of feline, not one to be cowed by cows, made to feel sheepish by rams, unresistingly badgered by badgers.

"Am I a man or a mouse?" he asked himself, and his reply comforted and encouraged him. "I am neither. I am a cat!"

Yes, he was Pushkin and no more need be said.

He walked all night and went into a trance so that the distance became the detritus of a dream, the miles dispersed behind him like smoke, and even though his exhaustion was acute he kept going, following a particular star, following the point of celestial light, that distant sun, even when the clouds came together like spoilsport curtains and covered it from prying slitted eyes. He still knew where it was and was determined to use it as a guide.

But it wasn't the North Star and it moved gradually across the sky like all other stars, so the route of Pushkin's voyage was actually a gentle curve over the landscape that only *felt* like a straight line.

Then the stars began to lose force as if they were suffering from twinkle fatigue and they dimmed and the sky grew lighter in the east, which was the east *because* the sky grew lighter there, and Pushkin found himself standing on a hill, more of a grassy knoll really, looking down at a town, a town that wasn't Small Mercies. He hadn't gone in a giant circle.

But it wasn't Denial either and he didn't yet know that.

It was Shovekin, a strange place.

No roads led into this town, only mud paths that were baked hard or slimy and treacherous depending on what the weather did. At the moment they were a bit soft but not like linear quagmires. It had rained in the past week but it hadn't poured. No clouds had burst. Most of the water had been absorbed, drunk deep into the earth and only a few bubbles had been hiccupped back out, where they swirled around each other in the very narrow ditches on either side of the paths like liberated cuckoo spit, dancing waltzes.

As he walked down the hill, refreshed by the sight of the town despite the rigours of his journey, his tail held high, Pushkin heard the solitary whining of a dog rising like sonic smoke above the chimneys of the houses, and he felt a little fear but decided to suppress it and continue.

The dog in question was standing at the end of the path and he was clearly guarding the space between the town and the rest of the world on this side of the compass, not that he really knew what a compass was. Pushkin stopped when he caught sight of the big brute, but the dog's nose twitched a few times and his tail began wagging and then he said jovially:

"Good morning! Have you come to live here too?"

"You can speak!" gasped Pushkin.

The dog rolled his eyes in mock alarm. "So can you!"

Pushkin relaxed and purred.

"I am looking for my owners," he explained.

"Your owners?" said the dog.

"They vanished yesterday. I think they ran away from an acquisitive bear. I am searching for them. Are they here?"

"Your owners, you say?"

"My owners are Bethan K. Fullfor and Tommaso."

"Your *owners*! Ha ha!"

"Why are you laughing at me?" asked Pushkin.

"I'm not laughing at you but at your naivety. Don't you know that you are their owner, not the other way around?"

"No, I didn't know that," admitted Pushkin.

The dog continued, "Human beings are the rightful pets of animals. That's the way nature intended it to be, that's how it works, but this truth seems to have been forgotten in most parts of the world."

"How do you remember it?" Pushkin wanted to know.

"Because this town is Shovekin."

"What difference does that make?" persisted Pushkin.

"A big difference, believe me."

"Won't you reveal what I ought to know?"

The dog took a deep breath and said, "It often happens that human beings move house and forget to take the animals that share their homes with them. The animals are forced to set off on long voyages in order to find those humans. It is not uncommon for them to find this place instead, Shovekin, the town where the rightful order of things is preserved. For example, you have found it. Here, dogs and cats and all other animals are in charge and men and women are their pets. I am glad you have found your way here."

"You are inviting me to join your community?"

The dog bowed, bending its front legs until its noble head nearly touched the ground, then it straightened. "Yes."

Pushkin licked his lips. "May I look around first?"

"You may indeed. Follow me."

The dog led Pushkin into the town. It looked similar to Small Mercies and the streets and buildings were almost identical. Cats and dogs walked along the pavements and many were leading humans on a leash. Sometimes those animals were in a hurry, perhaps on their way to an important meeting, but their humans would stop to greet other humans, shaking hands and discussing the weather for ages, until the exasperated animals would jerk the leash and pull them apart and set off again at an even more rapid pace.

They passed a garden in which swung a cage from a tall pole and in the cage was a man. He was unable to stand up or stretch himself and he seemed to be very unhappy imprisoned like that. He was dressed in an expensive business suit that was frayed and creased, but a parrot was perched on the top of the cage and was calling down through the bars:

"Johnny wants a salad? Who's a clever adult then? Pretty Johnny, pretty Johnny. Can you say that? Pretty Johnny."

The man in the cage mumbled something unintelligible.

"What was that, Johnny? What are you going to offer me for a salad? Do you want to make me an offer, Johnny?"

"Stocks and shares," croaked the helpless prisoner.

"Good *businessman*," said the parrot.

"It might seem cruel, but apparently humans don't have souls, so it's not at all cruel really," explained the dog.

Pushkin was very impressed by the fact there was no motorised traffic on any of the roads. Humans that had been let off the leash frolicked in the middle of the street, brewing tea right there and reading newspapers, all the silly games they enjoy so much. "Amazing," he said.

Further along, two hedgehogs were nailing a human into a box. This was because it was that person's hibernation time. Then they passed a man who was wearing a uniform and cap and was standing to attention behind a gate. "Do you have an appointment?" he snapped at them.

"What did he ask me that?" said Pushkin.

"Oh, he's just a guard human. Some animals keep them to deter intruders and burglars. Do you like this place?"

"It's like paradise," replied Pushkin.

"We will give you a house and you can choose a pet from the abandoned humans' shelter if you feel the need for one."

"Assuming I'm accepted into the community?"

"I feel confident you will be."

"I think I adore this place already."

The dog nodded. "Good. All that remains is for me to introduce you to the ruling committee of the town. All of us found our way here after our pet humans moved house and left us behind."

"Humans really are rather stupid," said Pushkin.

"That's why we love them so!"

"Yes, yes, I suppose it is. But there's one thing."

"What is it?" asked the dog.

"I do miss Bethan and Tommaso. It wouldn't feel right having any other pets. The substitution would be inadequate."

"You never know. You might still get them back."

"How is that possible?"

The dog flung a paw around Pushkin's shoulders and in a conspiratorial voice said, "Where do you think all the humans who live here come from? They dwell in their distant towns for only a short time before they wake up to the fact that their 'pets' are missing, that they forgot to take them along in the move. So they get frantic and start searching for them and frequently they end up here, in Shovekin, reunited with their beloved animals but with the proper relationship restored between them. In your case—"

"No," said Pushkin sadly, "I don't think my humans will do that. There is something a bit peculiar about them."

"Humans can be incomprehensible. Ah well! You can only wait and see. Incidentally, I haven't introduced myself formally yet. I am Shako. Follow me and I'll present you to the committee."

And he trotted down a narrow alley and through a hole in a fence. With a spring in his step, Pushkin kept close behind.

Bethan finally had her hunch but it didn't help her to work out what was missing and to be honest the hunch didn't suit her. So she removed her cardigan and the hunch fell out. It was a large purple pillow and it landed on the floorboards with a satisfyingly plump and comfy sound.

Bethan bent forward and stared down intently but she wasn't scrutinising the pillow. It was the varnished floorboards she was more interested in. Why did they seem *wrong*? They were smooth and shiny and unscratched. Was there any clue in the fact of their pristine condition to help her decide why this new house had an inferior atmosphere to the old?

"Tommaso!" she bellowed. "Tommaso!"

He came running, slipping on the polished wood in his pink slippers and struggling to untie the knot in his apron.

"Yes," he panted anxiously.

She knitted her brows, the only thing she ever cared to knit. The task of darning socks in this domestic setup was done by him. "Do you still think we might have left something behind us?"

"I have learned not to attempt to think."

"Idiot! I am ordering you to do so *now*. Tell me, did we forget something when we moved from Small Mercies?"

He visibly seemed to shrink, but his mind was working; his ears glowed as they always did when cogitating. "Could it be," he ventured mildly, "that we didn't bring the cat along with us?"

"Pushkin, you mean? Don't be absurd!"

"It's just that I haven't seen him around lately and in fact I don't think I have seen him since we arrived here."

Bethan folded her arms under her bosom, threw back her head, laughed at the ceiling until the ceiling started to get paranoid. "You are most amusing, dear, like a mediaeval clown or jester. Like a fool. You *are* a fool, aren't you? A silly and pointless buffoon. But that's why I value you. I would have sold you years ago to the slaughterhouses or into slavery if you weren't so darned entertaining. Annoying, certainly, but in a good way."

"Thank you." He curtsied somewhat clumsily.

"However," she continued, and her tone became icy, "there's a time and a place for everything; and right now *isn't* the time for humour. So be sensible and answer my question properly or you will be horribly mutilated by these hands of mine. Look very close." And she lifted them up like solid yeti footprints in front of his pale face with its quivering muscles.

"I can't think of anything that might be missing," he said.

93

"Good." She nodded vigorously.

Tommaso noticed the pillow on the floor and he squatted to retrieve it. He was in this position when Bethan suddenly rested her hands on the crown on his head, preventing him from rising again.

"It couldn't be the cat. How could it be? We still put out cat food and it is eaten. That proves Pushkin is still around. Or are you going to suggest that *other* cats come in at night illegally to devour it?"

"You know best," he said.

"Yes dear, I do. I see you have found my hunch. It's your turn to wear it. If you take it off without permission I will have you sent to the recycling depot. I want you to shout 'the bells, the bells' at intermittent intervals until I tell you to stop. Do you understand? Do you?"

"Yes, yes, anything you say, anything at all!"

She removed her hands from his head and strolled over to the window and gazed into the garden. They would never go in search of Pushkin because as far as she was concerned there was no need and Tommaso wouldn't dare disagree with her. In fact he was now equally convinced that Pushkin still resided with them. Unlike many other couples they would never set off on the quest to locate their absent cat and they would never stumble across the town where he was. He simply wasn't missing in the first place.

There was a logical reason why they had this attitude.

They were living in Denial.

Fifty Cups of Lady Grey

1. Grayson was a cat with grey fur. His owner was a little grey woman with tangled grey hair who lived in a grey house in a grey town under the greyest of grey skies.

2. In a grey world the absence of vivid colour means that aromas and sounds fulfil the function of the visible spectrum. Musical scales and perfumes are rainbows.

3. Grayson's nose twitched. Someone was brewing tea again.

4. There were servants who occupied the same house. A very old butler named Eldon who wore a jacket with three sleeves and moved his boneless arms so rapidly it was impossible to tell which sleeve was empty; and an even older butler named Gak who wore a mask carved to resemble the head of an owl.

5. Or maybe his face really was like that?

6. The butlers took it in turns to brew tea. They used a teapot so large that it served them as sleeping quarters when it wasn't full of boiling water.

7. They always made more tea than was strictly required. They still believed that one day the house would be so full of guests that the teapot would be drained to the dregs. They lived in anticipation of that occasion. Or maybe they never really believed it deep down. Perhaps it was only Colette who did.

8. Colette was Grayson's owner.

9. It was never cold inside the house but it always felt cold. It felt cold because the flames of the fire in the hearth were grey. It was easy to be tricked into putting a hand into that fire because it seemed so harmless and bland. But grey burns are as bad as any.

10. Colette rocked endlessly on her grey rocking chair, back and forth, forth and back, and the creaking she made somehow was less grey than anything else in the room. It was a dull brown. That is why she never ought to stop.

11. The scent of the tea continued seeping through the bare grey floorboards from the kitchen below and the scent was a pale blue and it combined with the brown of the creaking to produce a strange hue unknown in nature.

12. But it was a colour that was not grey and that is all that mattered to Grayson.

13. A muffled shout far beneath suggested that Eldon or Gak had fallen into the teapot again. They often did that. The shout was half despair and one third perverse joy. It was also one sixth bewilderment.

14. They improved the flavour, Colette maintained, as they splashed about trying not to drown.

15. The butler who hadn't fallen in would be compelled to go off and fetch a rope from somewhere in order to rescue his companion. There were many ropes coiled and waiting in cupboards all over the house and they were all grey and frayed.

16. On those rare occasions when Eldon and Gak fell into the teapot together, the combined cries of both men would rouse a third butler, Hissburton, from his state of suspended animation on a shelf in the least frequented pantry at the back of the kitchen. Very slowly he would stir and fetch a rope of his own in order to rescue the younger butlers.

17. Never had all three fallen in. That would have been the end of them. Hissburton was so old he regarded apes as modern and bone flutes as futuristic. He thought that ropes were the nostril hairs of monsters and they always made him sneeze.

18. He shook with fear whenever he saw Grayson, believing him to be an enormous grey bear in the distance rather than a domestic cat at close quarters. There were no small felines in the world of his imagination, only the tigers and panthers than had eaten his parents.

19. Colette preferred it when Hissburton was in hibernation.

20. The servants were ponderously slow but they always tried to fulfil their duties correctly; or if not correctly, after falling in the teapot, then wetly. The grey grandfather clock in the grey alcove of the greyest room of the grey house was the witness to their determination and precision as they passed back and forth, forth and back, through the interconnecting chambers and passages.

21. The owl mask that Gak wore sometimes swivelled on his neck even though the head beneath remained still.

22. If Eldon had made his empty sleeve swing from left to right, right to left, and kept regular time with it, the pendulum

of the clock would have been jealous, but he never did, and it never was.

23. A real grandfather had once occupied that alcove. Nobody knew why he had vacated it or where he had gone to. It was even a mystery as to who he was the grandfather of. Presumably it was someone.

24. Colette had grandfathers of her own and they lived in sheds on their allotment gardens. They had plots next to each other but never grew anything edible because the ground consisted of voracious grey quicksands. Once they had attempted to dump many tons of grey flour into the bubbling mass and stir it with extra long spades. The plot thickens. The plots thicken.

25. But no, they did not.

26. Grayson knew that the butler who had fallen had now been rescued. The tea was almost ready. It would come up on the shoulders of the servants, borne like a sedan chair on poles. Biscuits would follow.

27. The sound of a grey biscuit being dunked into a cup of grey tea was a lemon colour.

28. Coincidentally lemon peel was one of the ingredients in the only blend of tea that Colette drank. But it was the peel of grey lemons. Orange peel, also grey, was another.

29. Oil of bergamot, cornflower and lavender were three other ingredients and all were grey, and even the black tea they flavoured was not really black but grey, and the grey beverage that resulted from this mixture, served in grey cups on grey

saucers and tasted by grey lips, was graceful and great, qualities that are acoustic variations of grey.

30. Grayson rose from the grey cushion on which he had been napping and stretched his grey body. Then he jumped down onto the floor and padded quietly towards the open door, his paws smudging the reflected grey flames of the grey fire in the grey hearth on the polished grey boards.

31. Today was a special occasion; or rather it *would* be a special occasion. That at least was the big idea.

32. Grayson passed under the rocking chair as Colette continued to make the colour brown with its creaking. He timed it perfectly and his tail wasn't crushed. Then he passed out of the room and paused at the top of the stairs that led down to the subterranean kitchen.

33. He rapped a paw on the base of the highest baluster of the bannister and the sound vibrated up the strut and down the wooden rail to the carved figurehead at the very bottom; and each rap emerged from the open mouth of the worn grey gargoyle with amplified force, as if the hideous beast was clucking its tongue.

34. Grayson counted as he rapped.

35. When he reached a particular number he walked away, tail swinging, and began a journey.

36. It would take approximately one hour, that journey, and all of it would be indoors, an odyssey entirely within the house, a domestic anabasis from the grey familiarity of the

greyest room to the enigmatic upper floors of the rambling mansion where even the dust motes were reluctant to go.

37. Grayson was tolerant of pathetic fallacies. Therefore he felt a degree of sympathy for those motes.

38. Far below, Eldon and Gak were frothing with excitement as they opened cupboards and took out the required quantity of china cups. Even Hissburton stirred in his sleep as the intensity of their joy communicated itself through the cobwebs of his hibernation.

39. The most mysterious butler of all was the object of Grayson's search. This butler was older even than Hissburton, older than prehistory and the origin of the universe, so old that a time loop was involved and he actually came from the future. Or so the story went.

40. This story.

41. It is better not to believe everything you read. But better for whom? For you, perhaps. But only perhaps.

42. Colette continued to rock and as she did so her tongue swung in her mouth from hollow left cheek to hollow right cheek, right to left, in time with the chair and the pendulum of the grandfather clock and the sleeve of Eldon, had Eldon been a different kind of butler, and she suspected nothing, her mind was empty.

43. Like a teapot about to be filled.

44. Grayson found what he was looking for. To rouse the oldest of all old butlers he had to climb inside him and manipulate internal levers with his paws.

45. Eldon and Gak now had the correct number of cups arranged on a large tray. They would leave the tray in the kitchen while they carried up the giant teapot and then return to fetch it.

46. They attached the sturdy poles to the harness, secured the harness to the teapot, tightened the straps in the buckles and hoisted the poles onto their shoulders. Neither of them had noticed that the teapot lid was missing.

47. Grayson began his return journey, the opposite of his anabasis, from the upper floors to the greyest room, and this voyage was his *katabasis*, but he no longer had the appearance of a cat. He was Perry now, older than stars, more crooked than a solidified whirlpool, simultaneously unborn and eternal.

48. The full teapot was so heavy and the stairs so steep that its progress was excruciatingly slow. Perry entered the greyest room before Eldon and Gak had reached the highest step. He leaned over the shoulder of Colette and gibbered in her ear.

49. Her shriek was the loudest shriek recorded anywhere that year in any of the towns of the region. She made no attempt to jump out of her chair but merely leaned forward and rocked it much harder so that it accelerated across the floor and out of the door to the top of the stairs, where it tipped her into the teapot that Eldon and Gak were bringing up. Hissburton appeared with the lid and clamped it down tight. The tales that her grandfathers had told her were true after all...

50. Or were they? Grayson climbed out of the costume and Perry ceased to exist. Back down they all went and the tea was perfectly flavoured by the time they stood near the tray of fifty cups. They poured and began drinking. One, two, three... And the colours were so bright and durable they finally painted the world permanently and made it a better place.

Rhys Hughes was born in 1966 and has published 27 books and written 720 short stories in the past two decades and his work has been translated into ten languages. He is a confessed cat lover. When not writing or admiring cats, he spends his time mountaineering, dabbling with music or lazing around. To find out more please visit: http://rhyshughes.blogspot.com

The illustrations in this book are all by different artists. These artists are as follows:

Page 06 – **Colin Langeveld**. Science Fiction and Fantasy book illustrator. Published mainly in Europe.

Page 08 – **Chris Harrendence**. Illustrator who lives on a Welsh hillside, just past the middle of nowhere. He shares his hillside with his family and an overweight cat.

Page 29 – **Bob Lock**. Welsh writer of SF/Fantasy/Horror, also, part-time cat wrangler.

Page 49 – **Adele Whittle**. Creator of miniature paintings inspired by nature on pebbles, sea slate and sea glass, including art you can wear! http://tiddushop.blogspot.com

Page 55 – **Fiona Duffin**. Born in Australia but grew up in Africa. She has been drawing cartoons since the age of 5. She now lives and works in London.

Page 59 – **Angus Fergusson**. Lives alone, upstairs in a Dickensian Kent apartment block and is now a cartoonist. His favourite subjects are angels and dogs.

Page 70 – **Paulo Brito**. Born in Arcozelo (Braga), Portugal and began writing poetry at the age of 15. Still writes, but mainly short stories, for the sake of mental hygiene.

Pages 4 & 102 – **Mariana Tavares**. Lives in Lisbon. Some of her drawings and paintings can be seen on her blog: http://marianarute.tumblr.com